S0-BIH-372

Heart of a Gorilla

Heart of a Gorilla

Stephen Robbins

Published by:
Buffalo Commons Press
P. O. Box 525
Dickinson, ND 58602-0525

In conjunction with:

Old Mountain Press, Inc.
2542 S. Edgewater Dr.
Fayetteville, NC 28303

www.oldmp.com

Old Mountain Press

© 1998 Stephen Robbins
Cover illustrations by Andy Robbins
ISBN: 0-9656007-0-X
Library of Congress Catalog Card Number: 98-96736

This book is a work of fiction. Names, characters, places, and incidents either are products of the author's imagination or are used fictitiously. resemblance to actual events or locales or persons, living or dead, is entirely coincidental.

Heart of a Gorilla.
Printed and bound in the United States of America. All rights reserved. Except for brief excerpts used in reviews, no portion of this work may be reproduced or published without expressed written permission from the author or the author's agent.

First Edition
Manufactured in the United States of America
1 2 3 4 5 6 7 8 9 10

For My Parents

Lee and Lorene Robbins

Acknowledgments

I wish to thank Donna Camoesas and Amy Kraus for their sharp editing and proofreading skills and for suggestions and ways to improve the manuscript. A special thank you to my son Andy for his cover art and to Tom Davis of Old Mountain Press for his advice and guidance. Of course, any errors are my own.

Heart of a Gorilla

To Hal Haynes—
a fun colleague—
hard worker and
juggler of many jobs and
tasks on the Dicikinson
State University circus
train —I've really
enjoyed working with
you.

Best
Steve Robbins
Jan. 1999

37
550

Overheard in a Barrel

I still have a photo of myself, taken in Garden City that summer in 1914 when we were trouping across Kansas with the thunderstorms and wind. The misfit *was* a misfit. Sammy Starr. Samantha Puluski.

Snapped in one of those brick buildings with the high tin ceilings, the photo shows me dressed in my polka dot clown costume without any makeup: a tall fifteen-year-old girl with straight, short blonde hair parted in the middle of her forehead, one side of it flipped back over one ear. Then my eyes were green with flecks of brown floating in them. In the photo, my face is angular, the chin slightly pointed, with a dimple, and the cheekbones high and pronounced. My nose is straight, the nostrils flared. My jaw is set and my lips tight, a thin angry line over white teeth.

Now I call that pose the old Sammy Starr, the lonely clown challenging the camera with a bit of false bravery and naivete and determination in her stare. But the photographer snapped that picture before I started to "see the gorilla," an expression I first began to think about in Garden City, after Joey trapped me in a barrel.

The memories begin when Joey the Midget and I were practicing between shows under the Big Top one hot, lazy Kansas summer afternoon. Above us the trapeze hung empty, and the blue sky flicked through some holes worn in the top's canvas. Outside, Old Satan the lion growled in the menagerie tent, and somewhere a barrel clanked against metal.

"Sammy, you've got to get this gag. Feel it," Joey said, wiping his head with a red bandanna and glancing across the ring as a workman led a brown pony past the front entrance. Joey's head came up to my waist. He wore a pair of bib overalls with the pants cut off at the knees, a scuffed pair of leather shoes, and a faded pink shirt. Beads of sweat rimmed his bald head.

"Okay, midget." I was tired and hot.

"Don't call me midget. I ain't some noxious insect or a freak. Grow up. You're sounding more and more like the Colonel."

"I'm sorry."

"You're forgiven. Now pay attention. It'll knock'em down. It's all in the timing." He pointed at the large red metal drum with its handle and wheels painted yellow. He had stenciled *Spot Remover* in white and black letters on the barrel.

"I understand it, Joey. I fall when you're chasing me, and you roll over me, stop a minute to do—"

"To tie my shoe. You're not listening."

"Right, and then I crawl up on the inside, slide out the cutout, hold on, and you roll me out and leave a flattened shadow of myself. It's pretty easy, really."

Joey's heavy face sagged into a frown. "Then practice it again. You can't be a star unless you're perfect, and only perfection will make these rubes laugh."

"It's too hot," I said. The air felt heavy and moist like wads of wet cotton. Even the guy ropes anchoring the canvas weren't flapping, and heat waves shimmered down off the white and blue canvas. It felt like we were toasting on the inside of a giant peanut roaster.

"Maybe it'll rain tonight," Joey said. "Get it right this time and then we'll stop." He pointed a stubby finger at the barrel and smiled, showing crooked teeth.

I lay in the dust, smelling crushed grass and sawdust as Joey rolled his barrel over me. I opened the door, climbed inside, dropped out the black cloth cutout of myself, closed the door, held

9

on to the inside handles, and waited for Joey to imagine he was tying his shoe.

Soon I was spinning upside down and round and round, heading for the short distance to the entrance. Then, the barrel stopped, and I was right side up, sitting with my back against a cushion I had strapped in the barrel to protect myself. Because the trap door was beneath me, I waited for Joey to roll the barrel another half turn before I could climb out. I expected to hear Joey cracking some joke at my expense. He didn't, and through my large mesh-covered peep and air holes I saw why.

Now out of the tent, he was waddling on short legs toward the shade of a parade wagon, looking like a satisfied duck heading toward a pond. He turned and looked over his shoulder at the barrel.

"Midget, eh? I'm sick of that name, and don't you forget it. Family don't talk to each other that way," he yelled at me. Then he grinned, said something to someone, slapped his hands on his legs, and jumped up and down, laughing.

Although I immediately thought of tossing him into the snake cage, locking the door, and dangling the keys before his terrified eyes, I knew he was right. We needed to act like family because we were a family, all of us:Joey the Midget and Sammy Starr; the peanut and candy man with a bad leg; the World's Largest Fat woman with her dark mustache that she carefully shaved behind closed doors; even Satan the Lion, dreaming of forgotten hunts.

I wasn't going to give him the pleasure of hollering, of sharing his joke with the others, because I didn't want to hear about it a million times on Clown Alley where we dressed, so I kept quiet and vowed never to insult him again. Humbled, I waited for him to return.

Fortunately, the barrel rested in the shade of the tent and I sat upright, looking out of my prison at our parade wagons and white thunderheads mushrooming over the circus like billowing, giant midway tents.

I dozed off. At first the voices sounded far away.

"This circus needs a good gorilla." I recognized the high-pitched voice of Colonel Bob Thackerby, the circus's owner, standing above the barrel.

"A what?" The voice belonged to the band leader called the Trumpet, a short, older man with slick black hair and bowed legs who had yelled at so many bands that his voice sounded permanently strained. "I can't think of any good reasons to get one."

"I can." Colonel Bob's voice sounded slightly irritated. He was a smart man and planned ahead to run a good circus. Sometimes the people working for him caused him a lot of unnecessary problems by not going along with his ideas, but I liked them, at least most of them.

"Why?" Now that the Colonel was really peeved, the Trumpet toned his voice down an octave.

"It'll bring in the crowds. Not every circus shows a gorilla. Look at us," the Colonel said, thumping the top of my barrel with his hand, making it hum and vibrate. "We call ourselves Colonel Bob's Incredible Circus, Menagerie, and Wild West Show—The Greatest Train and Wagon Show in the World. How can we possibly live up to that title without a gorilla?"

"A lot of shows call themselves the greatest, and they still don't show any monkeys." The Trumpet should have guessed that the Colonel was reciting only arguments he'd rehearsed to himself for a long time. He always thought ahead.

The Colonel laughed, his short, satisfied laugh. "You're right about that. A lot of them just use the titles, but they're still the same old mudshows, dragging from podunk town to podunk town, from sorry county fair to sorrier pumpkin harvest."

The Colonel paused. Through the peephole, I could see only one white buckskin-covered leg and black riding boot, but he must have stood straight, surveying the row of tents in the hot sun, businesslike and majestic-looking at the same time. "Look at us. We might think we're the greatest too, but we're still pretty much a darn mudshow. We need to progress. To earn that dandy billing."

The Trumpet coughed into his hand like he was clearing his taps. "So we aren't the biggest attraction in America. But we still manage to bring 'em in."

"Now. But what about the future?" The Colonel's voice changed, sounding more solemn, more understanding. "America is competition. America is growing, is restless energy. Since we took the land from the Injuns and corralled the buffalo, we've been changing. We're getting bigger, ready to take the American Dream overseas, to plant Old Glory on foreign shores, to teach those little yellow Japanese some English. Nope, we need a gorilla for business, and I know where there is one."

"Where?" The Trumpet's voice squawked like his sour notes.

11

"About two hundred miles from here. In Scott City. On a farm."

"A farm?"

"Yup. Some traveling show dumped him a couple of weeks ago. Now the amusement's worn off, the farmer doesn't know what to do with him." The Colonel snorted. "He'll sell him for a reasonable price."

"A gorilla on a farm? In Kansas? He must be sick. Gorillas don't last long. Nothing lasts long in Kansas. Except the heat." He laughed harshly.

"Yes, in a barn. And I want him in Colonel Bob's Incredible Circus, Menagerie and Wild West Show—The Greatest Train and Wagon Show in the World, so after this show, we head toward Scott City and that barn."

"And leave the train?" The Trumpet's voice flatted.

"It'll save us some money. How else are we going to do it? We'll loop away from the Santa Fe and play towns we've never seen. Places that have never seen sawdust before."

"Leave the train? That's sort of . . . of not progressing."

"For a couple of weeks let's try a wagon show. Play in some new territory away from the larger places."

"Become a mudshow again?"

Even though I heard the Colonel step away from the barrel, his voice rose louder now. "No, a wagon show. We'll leave the train long enough to go to the Scott City County Fair, set up for a couple of days, pick up the monkey, play a few more county fairs, fall back to the train, head east for Missouri for the fall." The Colonel and the Trumpet were walking away, their voices fainter. "So find me someone who knows something about an ape."

I wasn't going to tell him I knew a lot about gorillas—too much.

Making Progress

Colonel Bob's Incredible Circus, Menagerie and Wild West Show—The Greatest Train and Wagon Show in the World stretched along the road, between two rows of elm trees, miles of cut wheat, and fields of sun-baked corn, thirsty leaves drooping. Beside the road, the dry Cimarron River looped around islands of white cottonwoods, the white sand of the creek bed spilling into muddy pools.

I rode with Jacko, the circus's animal keeper, atop a green baggage wagon, headed for Scott City. Our wagon bounced along a rutted road, spattered with dry mud and loaded with ropes and canvas, pulled by four work horses which also doubled as medieval warhorses in the walk around, the spectacle that opened the shows. Behind us followed the snake den and the cat wagon, carrying Old Satan the African Killer, a dusty, toothless lion asleep with one tufted tail and limp paw hanging outside his bars.

"When will we get there?" I asked Jacko, the driver.

Jacko was a black man in his early sixties. A couple of months ago, Joey, Colonel Bob, and I had watched him wander down a railroad track and across the circus lot, another castoff in a rainstorm, wet, muddy, limping in a pair of broken-down boots.

When he saw the Colonel, Jacko clicked his heels together, snapped to attention, and saluted. The Colonel returned the salute, stepped into the rain, patted him on the shoulder, and walked with him toward the cook tent, their heads close together, the Colonel's hand resting on Jacko's shoulder.

Jacko's square hands jostled the reins a little to nudge Old Red along. "Not tonight. Have to camp out someplace before long. We're progressing." He squeezed out the word and glanced at me out of the corner of his eyes. "You like to camp out?"

I shrugged. "Not really."

"I do. Least I used to." His large head with gray hair topped square shoulders and muscular arms.

"So." Why can't most people just leave a person alone?

"That was before Shiloh and Ft. Lincoln."

"Shiloh?" Talking did beat watching Old Red's back and withers.

Jacko patted his leg and then touched a flat spot on his nose. "You probably noticed the limp. A bullet bounced off my tough hide. Sioux war club smacked me in the Minnesota uprising. Nearly a hair-raising experience."

"You kill Indians?" I asked, humoring him, but now I was interested.

"Mostly tried not to. I was a buffalo soldier out of Ft. Lincoln in the Dakotas." He patted his head. "They called us that because of our hair. Like a buffalo's." He frowned and raised his voice. "Personally, I never saw no connection."

After a while, I changed the subject. "Colonel Bob's right. We need to progress. This circus lacks something—energy. America's growing, and we need to grow with it."

"Manifest destiny, right?"

I waved my hand. "Look around you. At all the space. We need more industry, more buildings. America needs to expand."

"Plow the prairie up and build factories, huh?" He rolled his eyes upward and clicked through his teeth at the horses. "You just ain't seen that gorilla yet."

"I've seen plenty of gorillas," I said bragging, exaggerating.

"What you know about gorillas, girl?"

"I saw a gorilla grab Buddy Lasso through a cage and rip his arm off," I replied.

"You don't say."

"Yes. I worked for the Barnes Circus and helped Buddy feed a gorilla. The same gorilla they shot a year ago after it broke out of its cage."

Jacko shook his head. "You should've been in school."

"You mean in the orphanage." I'd revealed too much and knew it.

I waited and started again. "Sure gorillas are dangerous. But a circus needs them to bring in the customers."

"Well, I say progress costs."

"Things you don't need," I said. "All progress is that way. You lose some things and gain some."

"Like the Indians and buffalo?" Jacko asked. He looked at me and didn't blink. "Or the slaves? Or school for that matter—or the orphanage?" He waved his hand vaguely.

I ignored his comment. "We'd draw larger crowds with the gorilla, and we'd make more money. Our salaries would go up." I didn't mention the danger of a caged gorilla. Anyway, I planned on staying out of Colonel Bob's sight and living in Clown Alley as much as possible. I certainly wasn't going to volunteer my gorilla knowledge.

Soon I forgot about the gorilla and our talk about progress as we drifted through the afternoon behind the plodding horses, dozing and nodding under the hot sun. Away from the corn fields and the creek bed, the prairie rolled away from us across the horizon like brown carpet, with occasional patches of grass and sunflowers near small springs. In one place, a prairie fire had burned across the land, blackening grass, gnawing into gullies and along the creek, charring cottonwoods into darkened skeletons. Jacko thought maybe a lightning strike had caused the blaze, and I argued that a hot coal from a passing train or a cigarette from a wagon had fired the land.

Now and then, we'd pass a farm house, its yards littered with rusting harrows and balers and broken-down wagons. Sometimes a woman dressed in a faded calico dress stood outlined against a ratty screen door, looking like a moth trapped against a kind of grill. Kids in dirty overalls and hardened faces ran around the farm machinery and lined a dusty ditch, staring up at us as we passed by, ready to raise their hands, seeing something they'd only dreamed about. That's one thing I like about the circus. For a few minutes, even for the most hardened people, it dabs away a little bit of life's ugliness and humdrum and gives them a make-believe family.

"Where's your home?" Jacko asked.

"I don't have one."

"Well, where are your folks?" He kept his eyes straight ahead.

"My dad's dead," I replied, remembering the dumpy clown who had worked for the Cole Brothers Circus and made people forget their cares and laugh for a minute at him and his make-believe problems. "He clowned for a circus."

"Oh. Your mother?"

"I don't know."

He clucked to the horses. "Most everyone knows where family is."

"Not everyone." I waited and thought about how much I could trust him. "I ran away from the circus after my dad died."

"Then the police put you in the orphanage?"

I nodded.

"And you ran away because you didn't like it and you still got circus blood and you's still on the run?"

My head bobbed again. For some people on the run from the law and themselves, circuses are hiding places, moving towns of misfits who shelter other misfits, safety nets for catching the down and out.

"What you running from?"

"Nothing. This is home for me now. Like a family." Some family, I thought. A family of misfits.

"Your folks named Starr?"

"*My* name is Starr. Sammy Starr." My real name was Samantha Puluski and my parents had come from Poland, the home of great circus performers.

"Funny name for a girl. You trying to act like a boy? Being important?"

"You've got a lot of a questions about my business. Mind your own."

"Fine. Just trying to be friendly."

Before the sun set that evening, we topped a knoll, the prairie spread out before us, the sky scarlet and flame-orange, the land an ocean of black lapping against the red, and black thunderheads stacked on the horizon, like massed cliffs. In the distance I could see the town, a tiny speckle of lights, shimmering, as if some stars had plopped out of space onto the prairie.

"That'll be Scott City," Jacko said, tiredly, shifting in the wagon seat. He reached down, pulled a worn jacket, a faded blue

16

one with yellow stripes on the sleeves, from between his feet, and draped it around my shoulders. I flinched but took it anyway. "Prairie'll cool down tonight. Tonight, we'll camp just outside of town. And tomorrow, 'watch your horses, 'cause here comes the circus.'"

A New Job

The next morning, after we had paraded down the one-block Main Street—bakery, grocery store, general merchandise store—and past the wooden grain elevators, I dropped by the menagerie tent before our first Big Top performance.

A cool breeze had sprung up, and Jacko had lined the animal cages—all five of them—up in a neat row. Old Satan lay stretched on his back, asleep with his tongue lolling out, his paws cupped in the air, his legs spread. Bobo, a black bear, his black tongue panting, squinted lazy eyes at two kids trying to crawl toward the cages.

Jacko was splashing water into a big metal kettle for gimp-legged Tom the Bobcat, which we advertised on colorful posters as Tom the Arkansas Devil Cat. A bootlegger had snared him in a metal trap, and the Colonel had paid ten dollars for him. Some of the water sprayed a mist, and from a corner the cat shook his head and lifted a front paw gingerly.

"Good afternoon, Sammy. Too hot for 'em." Jacko growled, glanced at the kids, and wiped the sweat off his face. "You'd think those kids never seen a common old Arkansas bobcat before. Must be the posters. We need some rain. Heat's worse on them than on us."

I followed him to the snake den. A couple of dusty pythons had uncoiled themselves and lay with their snouts against mesh breathing holes. Their eyes amber slits, they flicked dark tongues through the wire. The musky odor of snake washed out of the holes, an odd odor, like rotting squash.

"The Trumpet told me the Colonel's after a gorilla," Jacko said, motioning for the two boys to approach him. "That's a problem, a big problem." He scratched the gray stubble of his beard and looked worried. "How we gonna keep him? Healthy, I mean? They just don't last too long."

"They usually die in captivity."

Jacko narrowed his eyes at me. "You said you'd . . . "

"We don't even have a cage," I said, looking around the small tent.

Jacko handed the boys a large metal bucket, told them to water the horses outside, and promised them free tickets for the evening show. "We can always build a big enough cage. I'm just wondering what to feed him. I don't know anything about gorillas. He'll probably be sick when we get him."

"We used to feed The Old Man fruits and vegetables." I said it before I thought, and I knew I had made another mistake when Jacko paused, stopped peeling ham off a bone with a sharp butcher knife.

Jacko arched his eyebrows toward the top of the canvas. "You fed The Old Man? That killer monkey?" He sounded doubtful.

"Well, I mean I watched her mostly. I didn't really take care of her." I tried to cover up, but I knew Jacko was more interested than he acted.

"That a fact? Well, if we get this big ape, I could always use a hand." He eyed me down his long nose like someone sighting along a rifle barrel, adjusting his eyes on a distant target.

I didn't want anything more to do with animals, especially sick gorillas. "The joeys really need me in their gags," I replied, heading for the opening and Clown Alley, glad to escape Jacko's gaze.

That afternoon, painting my face and putting on my putty nose for the show, I had forgotten all about the conversation with Jacko. When we assembled outside in the backyard of the Big Top for the "spec," or grand entrance, I noticed the weather had cooled down.

In the north, a line of black thunderheads ribbed the horizon like furrows of freshly plowed earth. A light breeze lifted the red flag from the center of the Big Top's pole and floated the warm smell of roasted peanuts and buttered popcorn over a crowd of townspeople.

During the show, Joey and I worked our "blow offs" well, surprising the audience with our endings. From my peephole in the barrel, I watched as one red-faced man with gold-rimmed spectacles and a stiff, black collar over a stiff, white shirt laughed and wiped away the tears with a stiff handkerchief, when Joey picked the flattened shadow of me up from beneath the barrel. We watched the rest of the show in front of the main bleachers, throwing a few tricks in between acts.

After Tiny Legs' dog act, the Grande Finale began. Colonel Bob charged around the red-and-white ring on Old Charley, his white horse, waving his hands at the crowd. Dressed in white buckskin with a lot of fringe, the Colonel made Old Charley bow to the audience while he doffed his ten-gallon hat.

"Thank you for coming tonight, ladies and gentlemen and now for the most spectacular event ever seen in Dea . . . Scott City—a western extravaganza—Colonel Bob's Vision of America, our blessed land of progress."

Then from a side entrance, the circus's stagecoach, painted light yellow with red trim, careened into the arena, chased by fifteen blood-thirsty savages waving rifles and tomahawks.

"Blam. Blam."

The drivers shot back at the renegades. Passengers screamed from inside and waved their hankies for help. "Save us from the redskins."

"Kill 'em. Scalp 'um. Ugh Ugh Ugh." Indians shot old pistols and waved tomahawks. Tent workers trotted behind the stagecoach. I bet most people saw Indians and cowboys. The imagination polishes a lot of tarnished metal, makes outcasts into heroic cowboys with blazing six-shooters.

The firecracker flashed. "Boom!" A boil of smoke sprouted up from the sawdust like a dark mushroom.

Suddenly, the horses bolted, their ears tucked back, their harnesses clanking, looking for a way out of the tent.

"Grab the reins, Bill. Whooa!"

The driver stood up, slammed on the wooden brake handle and stretched the reins far above his head. Smoke rolled from the wheel brakes. Bill, a clown, rode close to the lead horse, grabbed at the reins and missed. Of course, the crowd clapped and laughed.

"Look at that crazy Indian, will you?" someone yelled from the stands.

The horses charged around the track once, thundering past me, eyes wild with fright, nostrils flared while the coach was wobbling from side to side. One of the coach wheels hit a barrel, skidding into a tent pole. The horses squealed, and the driver tumbled backwards, dropping his reins.

At the far end of the Big Top, the stagecoach lurched and barrelled at Joey and me and the bleacher sections behind us—and all of the kids stood and cheered. I couldn't move.

Then, seemingly from out of nowhere, Colonel Bob's white horse Charley sprinted across the center of the ring, jumped two clown boxes, and ran neck and neck with the lead horses. The Colonel, his long, white hair streaming behind him, leaned over, grabbed the bridle of one of the runaways and jerked the horse's head. Charley pulled away sharply to the right, with the Colonel tugging hard, arms outstretched. Just before it rolled into the crowd, the coach shot toward a side entrance and out into the dark, snapping a guy rope as it swooshed out the opening.

I could move. I rushed across the ring and out into the cool evening air as the band played the closing number, "America the Beautiful." The coach was stopped in front of a cotton candy stand. The horses were stomping, snorting, breathing hard, and shaking their heads, jingling their harnesses. The passengers were crawling out of the coach, shaking their heads, rubbing their arms and shoulders.

"Dadgum, dadgum," said Betty, patting the top of her head. She appeared as the World's Tallest Lady in the sideshow tent, when she stood on hidden stilts. "That about piled my head through the roof."

"Shorten you up, all right." Tiny Legs, another midget, hopped to the ground and slammed his cowboy hat against a wheel. "My contract doesn't call for silliness." He stalked off toward the row of wagons. "I ought to blow this circus. That's a stupid act to do under canvas."

The rest of the passengers and some of the Indians stood around talking to Colonel Bob, who was patting the neck of his horse. "He'll be okay," the Colonel said, watching Tiny disappear into a costume wagon. "In life you've got to take risks. Can't think

21

little. Hah!" He raised his voice and laughed for the crowd's benefit.

Of course, Colonel Bob was right, and Tiny was wrong. A lot of circus acts bring danger—that's part of the appeal of the circus and that's why people pay to see trapeze artists, lion tamers, and runaway stagecoaches. They want to see Death right around the corner nodding in his hood and polishing his scythe, but they don't want to buy a ticket for a close up look. Tiny had peeked beneath the hood for a second and Death scared him, but Colonel Bob knew you needed Death dressed up, always there but disguised in the circus, hovering around the outskirts to bring in the crowds. Colonel Bob was a show man and brave.

He was talking to the others, calming them down, the center of attention, and waving his right hand a little, like he did when he was making a speech in the ring. I heard the word "gorilla," felt a funny feeling, and started to slip away for Clown Alley, wanting to hide out.

Someone yelled at me. "Hey, Sammy. Colonel Bob wants to talk to you." It was Jacko, motioning to me.

"I hear you know a lot about gorillas." The Colonel squinted his eyes, and I could tell he didn't recognize me behind the white paint and huge orange and green polka-dot bow tie I wore. "Well, speak up boy."

I disliked being called a boy, even by mistake. From anyone but Colonel Bob that comment would have brought an angry reply, but my respect for Colonel Bob was stronger than my pride. I idolized the Colonel and what he stood for, ideals of progress and self-improvement. To me, he led the circus. He was the circus, its symbol.

"I do, sir."

"Then, tomorrow I want you to go with Jacko to capture that barn gorilla." He laughed.

"What about my clown —"

"What's one clown more or less," he said laughing, winking and slapping his hand against the pearl handle of his six-shooter. He cackled again and elbowed Jacko in the ribs. "Tiny wants off the coach anyway. We wouldn't want to shortchange him. Hah! I'll use him as a clown."

Before I could think, I bobbed my head eagerly. "I'd like to go, sir."

"Good boy. I like your attitude."

He dismissed me with a flick of his head. "Well, ladies and gentlemen, let's close down for tonight." He started barking orders to the workers.

As I walked toward the clown wagon, I felt like I was floating above the dew-covered ground. People followed him so easily, and so did I. He was a natural leader because he stood for progress and the American way, just like the circus, I thought.

Sure, gorillas frightened me—terrified me, but if I helped Jacko out and stayed away from the gorilla as much as possible, then maybe the Colonel would notice me, even reward me with a bigger part under the Big Top. Maybe I could even sit on the stagecoach or ride a horse behind him into the ring. I'd have earned my identity in his eyes.

A Farmer's Barn

The next afternoon, after leaving Scott City at sunrise, Jacko and I bumped down a county road, headed for the Phelps farm. Before us, the road followed Shallow Water Creek, rising and falling over small hills and around maize fields, their stalks of grain heavy and brown in the clear sunlight. Meadowlarks chirped at us from the ditches, and red-wing blackbirds fluttered from cattails along the creek, aslant on brown stalks like black, musical notes. The creek widened and deepened and swung ahead of us and doubled back and turned over a heavy bridge. Our two horses clopped across planks and beneath rusted girders, and we pointed the horses' heads toward some distant buildings.

At the end of the road, the farm buildings lay tucked beneath some thick cottonwoods, away from the creek on a smaller rise of ground. The road looped in front of a white house with a green roof and sagging porch and a big, red dog. White chickens hopped, fluttered, and scratched in the dirt around a narrow building, its windows mesh-covered.

A two-story barn, shaped like a giant gray tent with puffed-out sides and topped with a weathervane on a square cupola, reminded me of the Big Top. In front of it, a wheat thresher with rusted wheels and gears was an iron elephant, marching toward the double-sliding doors, its square top the howdah for the rider.

As we stopped in front of the house, an older, white-haired woman and a man with a pot-bellied stomach dressed in khakis and blue suspenders stepped out of the house and walked toward the wagon. "You come to see about the gorilla?" she asked. She was wiping flour off her hands on a red apron.

"Can't you see that they're from the circus, Bessie?" the man asked angrily and jerked his hand toward the barn. "Keepin' 'em in there. Didn't want the thing in the first place. Fool gorilla."

The dog nuzzled her hand, and she patted the top of its head and rubbed him behind the ears. "I'll show you." She didn't look at her husband when she turned toward the barn.

Stepping inside the barn, I waited for my eyes to adjust to the darkness, my heart thumping in my chest. The sunlight from the door blocked a yellow rectangle of light onto the hay-covered floor, showing a row of wooden stalls on one side of the barn, bales of hay, rusty sickles and saws, dusty horse bridles and hames hanging from the walls like forgotten trophies. Along the south side, light filtered through windows and cracks in the wall. Through slots in an overhead hayloft, motes of dust drifted around us.

"It's back this way." The woman led us around some bales of hay toward the rear of the barn and toward a stall more brightly lit than the others. "I figured it was the best I could do. About the light, I mean," she said, nodding toward the stall and covering her chest with her hands. "I felt obliged, somehow . . . you know."

The gorilla lay on its side in a large cage on wheels, a hand outstretched in a pool of sunlight. The bars and darkness of the cage hid the huge form. Four black fingers of the hand flexed and tightened again, once, twice, as if they were caressing the light.

I squatted down to look in the cage.

The hand vanished. "Wraagh," the gorilla screamed weakly.

I screamed, lost my balance, and fell backwards, landing on my seat against a bucket filled with wagon parts.

"Devil," the farmer said. He picked up an axe handle near the cage and waved it in tight circles at the cage. "He's still got a little fight left in him. He quit eating on me. Should of shot him a month ago, but Bessie wouldn't let me."

The gorilla was quiet. I scrambled up and looked at Jacko. My legs were shaking, so I pinched my fingernails into my palms, hoping the pain would make the muscles stop. The muscles in Jacko's face tightened, and he stared at the farmer, the tendons in his neck jumping up and down like guy ropes from a tent popping in the breeze.

I just wanted to leave, to walk away, not to risk it. Our circus didn't need a mean gorilla, I thought, remembering how quickly The Old Man had snatched his trainer against the bars. I coughed, trying to get Jacko's attention, but he just stared at the farmer.

"Where'd you get him?" Jacko asked curtly, a skein of anger tightening behind his impatience.

"Feller came through here couple of weeks ago with a traveling freak show. Flat busted. Said he'd boughten him off a broke circus down south." The farmer popped his blue suspenders. "Got me some papers on him. That circus man needed the money to get down the road more'n he needed a fool gorilla."

"How much you want for him?" Jacko asked, pulling his heavy eyebrows together.

"Fifty dollars for the gorilla and ten for the cage." The farmer pulled at his suspenders again, his chest out, ready to bargain.

"Twenty for both," said Jacko and turned to go.

"No . . . I'd like . . ."

"We'll help you load it," the woman said.

The gorilla moaned softly once or twice as we moved the cage. I didn't look too closely at it as we pushed and dragged the cage down the row of stalls and under a thick chain and pulley and hoisted the cage into the back of the wagon. We covered the cage with a tarp, lashing it to the top, except for a space along the bottom of the cage, so air would blow in.

Riding back toward the circus, Jacko clucked softly to the horses and muttered under his breath, curses, soft curses. His hands shook while I held the reins for him as he lit a cigar, a long black Cuban one.

"Wouldn't been for the lady, he'd have died a long time ago," Jacko said, puffing smoke angrily at the grain elevators on the horizon. He glanced over his shoulder at the cage rattling in the back. "I'm surprised he's still alive. Didn't want to give up, I guess. Well, Colonel Bob's got his gorilla, but I don't know for how long."

If Colonel Bob wanted a gorilla to improve his circus, that was fine with me, I thought, but I didn't want to help Jacko nurse it back to health. "It'll probably die soon anyway," I said. "It's quiet, too sick to attack us now. But it'd kill us if we give it a chance."

After I helped Jacko drive the gorilla to the menagerie tent, I'd go back to the clowns, I thought. Soon I'd be under the Big Top, making the human race laugh at its own follies, hoping that Colonel Bob would notice my abilities and let me ride on the Deadwood Stage in the finale.

As the wagon bumped along, I glanced back at the cage. The gorilla was lying on its side, looking at me, its huge arms folded around a dirty iron kettle with water sloshing out of it. The water had stained the floor and wetted the black skin of his chest. It looked like he'd curled around it, trying to save it. His blue-black hair was matted filth, the fur tangled and wound into little balls of dirt, ribbons of neglect.

The gorilla was staring at me, his head on the floor of the cage, pressed against a piece of dirty newspaper. I knew he was sick: green mucus had crusted around his eyes, and flies buzzed around the top of his thick, sloping head. His eyes were open, brown, dull and filmed, staring unblinkingly at me. His mouth hung open a little, part of a black tongue showing, a yellow streak of teeth. Then, I noticed the lower part of his face, a white scar, the twisted lips and the scowl.

I turned away, fighting down the fear, my repulsion. As soon as we reached the circus, I would go to Colonel Bob and ask him to destroy it, put it out of its misery. The gorilla was too sick and dangerous.

The gorilla murmured a bit, like a dog that's hurt, but I didn't turn around.

I couldn't. I could think only about how The Old Man had wrenched the trainer's arms against the bars, how he had screamed in pain, my own fear, how I had been unable to move quickly enough to help him.

After a while, as the wagon rattled along, I asked Jacko if I could look at the papers the farmer had given him.

"Curious, huh?" he asked, handing me a large manilla envelope from beneath his feet.

I pulled out a handful of papers—legal forms, health certificates, one from the Congo, heavily stamped with circles and dates, some yellowing newspaper clippings, and a circus handbill from Barnes and Carson, depicting the gorilla looking fierce, his canine teeth biting into chains.

Jacko glanced at the papers as I shuffled through them. "Looks like he came from Africa, Sammy."

"No, *she*. The gorilla's a female. Yes, she did come from Africa," I said.

"Any name?" Jacko asked. Thinking, he rolled the cigar stub in his mouth and screwed up the bottom of his face.

"No, the papers—don't say."

I felt like telling him to turn the wagon around and go back to the farmer for his money. "Does it matter? She'll die soon anyway and Colonel Bob will lose his money."

"I guess it's his to lose. Tell me some more."

I searched through the papers. "Barnes sold her to a Tweetum Traveling Carnival and Tweetum dumped her on Uncle Jerome's Wildest Africa Menagerie in June. This gorilla'll hurt someone." I could hear my voice rising.

"Settle down, Sammy," Jacko said. Now on the outskirts of town, we bounced by a man hoeing a line of drooping tomato plants in his garden. The man lifted his hand in a half-hearted greeting, his wide hat a straw umbrella against the sun.

"She's still in her cage and sick." He glanced over his shoulder at the gorilla, eyes tightening, then looked at me, accusingly. "What happened to her face?" Jacko asked. He pointed towards the papers in my hand.

I searched through the documents, skimming them, reading quickly. "A sailor threw acid on her."

"What?" Jacko asked in disgust.

"When she was young. On her way to America. She didn't want to eat, so a sailor got mad and threw acid on her."

"He *what?*"

"It's what the newspaper clipping says. Listen to this." I read the clipping to him.

> This furious beast showed aggressive
> behavior even as an infant. Locked in her cage
> in transit to America, she tried to attack a crew
> member of the freighter. Frightened that she would
> break out of her cage, he fought her off by throwing
> acid at her.

Jacko shook his head in disgust. We both looked at the gorilla. She was asleep, her eyes closed, one hand still clutching the kettle, the fingers tightening and relaxing.

Jacko flicked the reins, muttering to the horse. "That's one tough gorilla. Acid on a baby," he said. He spit. "Same old story, now ain't it. Catch'em and brand'em. And then blame *them*."

The gorilla was still alive that night in the menagerie tent when I checked on her after the evening performance. Jacko was standing by the wagon, holding against his chest a brass lantern, which cast a warm circle of light on the cage, looking at her, lost in thought. He'd cleaned out her cage, scattering fresh hay in it. A pile of vegetables and fruit—oranges, bananas, cabbages, ears of corn—made a small pyramid beside a shiny, new water pail. The gorilla was asleep, breathing deeply, her back a humped shadow in the corner.

"How did you get in there?" I asked, nudging him.

"Through the door. But very, very quietly."

"I'd be very careful around her," I said.

He shook his head, his grizzled jowls shaking. "Sammy, she's too weak and sick." He sounded sad. Light from his lantern flashed off his gold tooth. "But she drank some water." He sounded pleased.

Outside, I could hear some of the yard crew talking and singing Negro spirituals as they pulled down the Big Top. The canvas rustled and sledge hammers clanked against stakes in heavy pings, jarring them loose from the ground.

"We're moving tomorrow. Early. Before sunrise." I looked at the cage. How would she survive if we moved her? I wondered.

"Yeah, I know." He scratched at his beard stubble. "I've thought about it already. You got a cot?"

"Why?"

"It'll be pretty easy." Jacko had his hands on his hips and was staring at me. "And you're the young lady to do it."

"Do what?"

"Take care of her." He squared his thick shoulders, saw the expression of disbelief on my face, and then shrugged. "It was the best I could do for her. With the Colonel." He bit off the name like he'd tasted a piece of rotten fruit. His eyes narrowed and he spat tobacco between his feet. "Either that or take her along."

I was speechless, and, believe me, Samantha Starr speechless is a rarity.

Jacko eyed me, waiting for me to speak, to hear my response. "I'm afraid she'll die if we move her," he said. I didn't like the serious tone of his voice.

"My job?" I asked. What would the clowns do without me in the gags? I didn't have enough money to camp out with a sick gorilla.

Jacko pulled some worn dollar bills from the front of his overalls and handed them to me. "Colonel Bob's money. It's not much," he said, "but you can buy some food with it while we're gone. For you and the gorilla."

"Where will we stay?" I asked, taking the bills.

"Here. On the fairgrounds in that old horse barn. They exhibit livestock there at fair time. I've already talked to the police chief and the local county fair committee."

A horse barn in Scott City, Kansas. My anger flared, and I felt sorry for myself. What kind of progress was this for Samantha Starr? Everyone was thinking about the gorilla, but I didn't seem to matter.

"What if I don't want to . . ."

"Think of it as an opportunity." He looked away from me. "Well, sort of," Jacko said, trying to console me. He patted me on the shoulder.

I pulled myself away. "Sure. Some opportunity," I said, sarcastically.

"Save the gorilla, and maybe Colonel Bob will pay you more. You'll get a promotion." He was trying to convince me, but his gravelly voice sounded doubtful.

I glanced toward the animal wagons, their doors shut for tomorrow's journey. I intended to hurt his feelings. "Just like you? For your military service with the 10th Cavalry in conquering the West with the buffalo soldiers?"

It was a hateful thing to say, and I was sorry after I said it. Jacko didn't say anything. In the silence, a couple of crickets screeched away like miniature violins out of tune, trying to follow each other's tiny scales, an insect duet. In his wagon, Satan the lion growled softly. I guess Jacko and I sounded like the crickets. I turned and started to leave, still feeling sorry for myself, but ashamed now of what I'd said to Jacko.

"Sammy. You could think of someone besides yourself, you know," he said after me.

I turned back. Jacko was clenching and unclenching his hand, staring in the distance, his face tight, muttering to himself something about a wounded knee. "*Some* conquest . . . Wounded Knee . . . why didn't I roll Hotchkiss . . . I didn't mean to . . ."

In the livestock barn that night, trying to sleep on my hard cot, its canvas stretched as tight as a drumhead, I thought of a lot of things. There I lay at the foot of the gorilla wagon, my stomach growling, wondering how long I would camp there, hungry, and still mad at Jacko for making me baby-sit a sick gorilla and upset that I hadn't said more to him—maybe something about his limp. Jacko had taken advantage of me. I'd made a mistake becoming too close, too friendly with Jacko. He was wrong and he'd used me. It reminded me of Old Maid Thompson at the Sunnyside Orphanage for Girls, always wanting me to smile and sit up straight in a starched dress.

So I lay there, vowing I'd never work another circus, planning on running away, but knowing I couldn't. I wouldn't leave the gorilla because even though I was mad I felt responsible to Jacko and Colonel Bob. Then in a few seconds, I'd imagine Colonel Bob rewarding me, as I presented him with a healthy gorilla, one that beat its chest and growled at the lines of paying customers.

"Thank you, Sammy," Colonel Bob would say. "Hop up next to the driver and grab that Colt .45." Samantha Starr, Center of Attention.

About two in the morning, by then on a white horse in Madison Square Garden, I drifted off into a strange dream. In some dark area, a fire was flickering and crackling somewhere just beyond my vision. Something soft touched me and covered me, protecting me. In front of the fire, strange shapes, shadows, moved back and forth, squatting and moaning, in a language I didn't understand.

Pickle Talk

Early in the morning, the strong smell of unwashed gorilla woke me. Overhead, barn pigeons cooed and fluttered in the rafters. I was wrapped up in my quilt decorated with horses, curled on my side. Someplace in the distance a dog barked a lonely, drawn-out howl. Light filtered through the cracks in the barn, cascading through the dust motes like gold bars. The gorilla moved in her cage and sighed and groaned softly.

"Trapped all right," I muttered. "Caught in my own big wooden cage along with a dying gorilla."

I rolled off the cot, stood up, dusted the hay off my work shirt and jeans, and looked at the cage setting on the wagon. The gorilla was lying on her side, watching me, her hand extended. I moved closer to the cage, my heart starting to speed up, like I was walking through tacks.

One hairy hand was touching a banana that she'd managed to inch away from the tomatoes and a yellowing head of lettuce. The tip of the banana was squashed, and mashed banana, a yellow paste, stained her fingers and palms.

"You'd like to do that to me, huh?" I asked. My voice sounded rough, out of place in the barn. "As if I'd give you half the chance. Ever, my friend."

As I stepped a little closer to her, she followed me with her brown eyes, her head motionless. A window behind me cast little squares of barred light into her brown eyes, and I could see the tiny shadow of myself stalking across her vision. Diamonds, I thought. The light reflecting from her eyes reminded me of diamonds. Black diamonds.

I stopped and stared at her, putting my hands on my hips. "Okay. We're not friends. Never will be. But we're stuck here for a while until you . . . uh, let's just make the best of it. I'll call you Black Diamond. My name is Samantha Starr. We're not exactly pleased to meet each other, huh?" She stared at me.

My stomach growled. Hungry, I turned away from her, thinking about pancakes and eggs at one of the small cafes across from the fairgrounds. Suddenly, I stopped, remembering her hand on the banana.

"Black Diamond, you won't let me close, will you?" I asked quietly, staring at the banana. "You'd grab me too. I'm going to eat. I'll be back."

A few hours later, Black Diamond didn't move as I climbed in the back of the wagon with the gallon milk bottle and a dozen bananas from Bill's Grocery and Meats and a piece of stiff, clear hose from Tony's Hardware and General Merchandise Store. Her eyes followed me as I mashed the banana in a cup and mixed the fruit with milk. I was nervous, very nervous, my arms shaking the way they do when you hold a heavy object too long in front of you.

When I first poked the hose through the bars, she jerked her head back, and bared her teeth. "Wraagh, wraagh, wraagh," she growled weakly. Her four large canines were as thick as white bullets. When she growled, she scared me so badly I nearly jumped off the wagon, dropping my hose inside her cage.

I tried again, this time pushing the hose slowly toward her, holding it above her head. She saw the hose and tried to move again, away from it, but she was too weak. I held the hose above her mouth and poured some milk and banana into my end of the hose. I watched the milk flow downward, my arms shaking and my heart pounding, thumping loudly, ready to jump off the wagon if she suddenly grabbed for me.

33

The milk flowed about halfway down the tube and stopped. "Good idea, Samantha, but you can't feed her this way. You need more height." I searched the barn and soon spotted a wooden egg carton against a milk separator. I hauled the carton back to the wagon.

Soon, milk dripped out of the tube and over her thick lips and down into the matted hair of her chin. Her dark tongue darted out and she licked at the milk and banana, slowly at first, then quickly. She made a funny sound, deep in her throat, like a baby crying far away.

"Samantha's Magic Gorilla Feeding Machine, huh?" I asked her. Again, standing on a box, peering down around the top edge of the bars, and guiding the tube back toward her open mouth, I poured the rest of the milk and banana mix down the hose. She drank most of it, then closed her eyes, and drifted off into sleep, her silver-dollar-sized nostrils quivering and her eyelids fluttering.

As I climbed off the wagon, I wondered if gorillas dreamed, and if so, about what? I also wondered what I was going to do until Colonel Bob returned on his way toward the railroad.

For a week, Black Diamond hovered between sickness and health. For three or four days, she lay listless in her cage, as if she'd given up. The flies crawled over her, and she didn't seem to have the strength to bat them off her face. On the fifth day, I checked her cage early in the morning, my heart in my throat, expecting to find her curled in death. But she was sitting in the middle of her cage, in a bar of yellow light, alert, her eyes clear and boring into mine.

"Yahoo!" I shouted. At the sound of my voice, three pigeons blasted off the barn floor and fluttered to high rafters.

She grunted.

"Good morning," I said and hopped on a bale of hay. "You're not going to die, and I now have a very large hairy problem. You're getting better, stronger, eating fruits and vegetables as fast as I can push them at you. But you're still not too friendly. I'm your feeder, nothing more. Wait until Colonel Bob gives me my reward."

A couple of days after that speech, the county newspaper discovered us and wrote a story about the circus leaving me behind to doctor Black Diamond back to health. At first she drew the town's people like iron filings to a huge magnet, but then after the novelty wore off they stopped coming except for a few kids, now and then.

But the story helped me—us, I mean. People really didn't know what to do with a four-hundred-pound gorilla, but they wanted to help, realizing that Black Diamond and I didn't want to camp out forever in their fair barn. They also realized that if the circus didn't swing by again they'd suddenly own a huge exhibit, one they couldn't show at the fall 4-H Fair.

Some people muttered disgustedly and talked about impeaching the mayor, and a few farmers in dirty overalls cussed and spat tobacco stains of hate in the dust, little round blobs of misunderstanding and ugliness. But mostly people were kind. They donated garden vegetables—tomatoes, corn, cucumbers, squash, eggplants—and field crops. I felt like a zookeeper as I took their gifts, thanked them, and kept them on the other side of a rope I'd strung in front of my hand-painted sign reading, "Man-killer. Keep a safe distance."

One day, a middle-aged woman even carried in some jars of canned, sour pickles, her cucumber, peace offerings. I tried to explain to her that Black Diamond loved green, fresh vegetables and milk and bananas and not sour pickles laced with chili peppers, but she insisted on giving Black Diamond a taste, and before I could stop her, she stooped under the rope.

"Oh, he'll just love it, dearie. It's Herbie's favorite recipe, and he's a real go—. Well, Herbie is a nice man, most of the time," she said. She hunched her shoulders, swung one heavy arm, red and muscular, and shot the pickle through the bars, grunting with delight.

Plop. The pickle slid against Black Diamond's leg.

Black Diamond looked at me, her eyes narrowing, and wrinkled her snout. "Wraagh?" The short grunt sounded like a question.

Then she picked it up and held it, curious, narrowing her eyes on it, black slits of distrust. She snuffed it, and her black tongue flicked over it once, lightly.

"Wraagh. Wraagh." Suddenly, Black Diamond lurched up, rolled onto her arms and front knuckles and bolted forward, her teeth bared, white slashes, slapping the bottom of the cage with the palms of her hands.

The woman's mouth dropped open; the open jar of pickles slid from her hand, hitting the floor; and juice splashed upward, shooting hot pickles over her lap. She toppled backwards over a bale of hay with her thick legs, her scuffed, buttoned shoes weaving overhead. I dropped to the floor like a clown had bopped me on the head with a huge rubber mallet, paralyzed with fright, a hot pickle mashed in my face.

Black Diamond grabbed some loose hay and threw it above her head, turned her back to us, and stalked to the back of the cage.

"Herbie never complains about my pickles this way," the woman said, peering over the hay bale, her voice a squeak. Her face was as white as a clown's whiteface. "He just eats them and never complains one little bit. Except to thank me. I mean he never eats them and just complains one little bit. I mean . . ."

She fainted. It took me ten minutes to prop her against the hay and to wake her up with a wet towel.

"I don't know why that gorilla don't like them pickles," she said, coming to and blinking her eyes. "That recipe won the Best of Show at the Annual County Fair."

"And doesn't Herbie just know it," I said.

After another ten-minute conversation about husband Herbie and pickles, she staggered out the door, angry at me for letting her feed a gorilla, blaming me for frightening her and threatening to go to the Women's Aid Society.

Black Diamond wouldn't face me the rest of the afternoon. I looked at her back, a black, thick arch in the cage, and thought about how stupidly I had acted in letting the woman too close to the cage and how she had looked, toppling over the hay, and what she'd said about her husband.

I almost laughed at the situation, but I felt like crying, and a vague idea that I couldn't express shadowed my mind, lurking in the darkness. I'm that way. Intuitive. Sometimes I'll feel an idea first, only sense the edges of it, before I can reason it out, explain it in words to myself and bring it into the light. Whatever was floating around in my mind, unnamed, concerned me in an irritating way, like a small rock in a shoe that bothers me when I walk, not hurting enough to make me remove it, but constantly poking me until I stop and take off my shoe.

"What is it?" I asked her. "We've been roomies in the barn about ten days now. You don't scare me anymore. I don't think you want to grab me. You're feeling a lot better now, aren't you? Your eyes are clear. Your coat's shiny. You eat about everything I push in your cage except of course eggplant, which you throw at me. But what's bothering me?"

Hot days drifted through warm evenings as we waited. Then late one evening, lying on my cot, listening to the barn creak around me, I was thinking about words, and I finally attached words to the idea that had been floating around in my mind. At last, I knew. I looked at Black Diamond's back in the gray light and realized she hadn't faced me all afternoon.

My heart jumped a bit. "Are you sick?" I asked. "What is it? Are you mad?" What had I missed or overlooked with Black Diamond?

She had acted like a gorilla. "She is a gorilla, stupid," I said to myself, poking a piece of straw at a purple-shelled beetle on the floor.

"But how should you behave?" I asked her. "At least you treat me better than the Pickle Lady. You didn't beat your chest, pull at the bars, and throw manure at me. You didn't act the way a gorilla ought to behave."

I thought awhile. "If I'm looking at you only in the way I'm suppose to see you, then maybe I'm seeing only what I expect to see and I'm not really seeing you."

"Okay," I said to her back. "I don't know how gorillas act or how they—you—talk." I pushed my mental pebble around some more. "Of course, you can't talk. You're a dumb animal, right?" Dumb means stupid, but it also means without voice, and I had known a deaf and dumb but very intelligent circus hand before. "I really didn't know how a gorilla acts, how you talk."

I stared at her back, but she wouldn't turn around. "You should have said something to me," I said to her. She didn't move. "Okay, be that way. Pout. It's not my fault she threw you the hot pickle. I just wish we could talk." I felt depressed and alone. I wanted to communicate somehow with her.

Then I remembered that before she'd picked up the pickle she'd looked in my direction and growled, but in a different voice than when she'd screamed at the lady.

Finally, I reached down and pulled the pebble from the shoe: understood and found the words for my idea. I said it: "All of us growl at each other. You, me, the Pickle Lady. Talk helps us to understand each other, but sometimes words and signs don't help much. Ever help. We cage ourselves away from each other.

"You have been trying to talk to me, in your way, haven't you? And I haven't been listening, because I've kept my ears and eyes shut to you." Suddenly, I felt embarrassed and upset, the way a person does when she knows she's hurt someone because she's ignored words, hand gestures, facial expressions—signs and signals—from that person.

"You're not the only one trapped in her cage," I said, now disgusted at my ignorance.

Reaching Out

After tossing and turning through the night, drifting in and out of sleep, trying to see dark figures on a sandy beach, I woke up the next day early, the sunlight firing the wood and hay in rose tints.

I cleaned out Black Diamond's cage with a long-handled broom, filled her tin pail with fresh water, and pushed some fresh vegetables and fruit toward her. She slurped the water with her face deep in the pail, and then she dipped her hands in the water and wiped the thick brow above her eyes, almost like she was combing her blue-black hair.

"No pickle dreams, huh?"

Black Diamond didn't even look up. She sighed and plopped down in front of the vegetable pile. She picked up an ear of corn, peeled away pieces of husk and stuffed them in her mouth, her heavy jaws grinding.

"Have a good night's sleep?" I asked, trying to sound as normal as I could talking to a gorilla. "You're still not mad, are you?"

As I was talking, Black Diamond was eating the white stem of a corn ear. She found another ear and peeled the husks away.

"What should I do next? Read you the Gettysburg Address? Okay, you can't talk and don't understand me. My words are only meaningless sounds to you. I'm trying to be friends. I'm tired of living as Sammy Starr the Gorilla Feeder Caught in the World's Largest Barn in Kansas."

So I talked away about the weather, about my dreams, about the number of rafters in the barn, until she finished her breakfast and started grooming herself, slicking down the hair on her arms.

Finally, I stopped talking, picked up a book about a circus veterinarian I'd found in the small public library off the courthouse, perched myself on a hay bale and started reading to her about care of circus animals-how to feed camels, move sick elephants, and pull thorns from tigers' paws.

Soon Black Diamond was dozing in the hot barn, slumped in corner of her cage, panting in the heat, her head nodding on her chest, her arms splayed out beside her. The words on the page blurred together, and I almost fell off the bale, so to wake up I decided to practice one of my clown gigs, the one where Joey swats me in the behind with a rubber shoe the size of a folded newspaper.

I was imagining Joey smacking me, and so for some reason I thumped my chest wildly and grunted, like a gorilla. Suddenly, Black Diamond jumped up and scooted to the front of her cage, scattering corn and tomatoes and green beans. "Wraagh. Wraagh." She bared her teeth and beat her chest, her eyes dilated. Pock! Pock! Pock!

Startled, I dropped to the floor, pressing my face down into the straw, slumping down, covering my head, my eyes away from her. I peeked at her from beneath my arm and watched her move away, stiffly, on closed knuckles, her rump in the air. The hair down the center of her back bristled like black nails. Her fists slapping her skin had sounded like distant drum signals, I thought. Messages. Suddenly, with my face buried in the hay, still shaking, I understood what I had failed to see before.

"You *are* talking to me," I said from the floor. "Aren't you? Except you're not using your voice. And I scared you with my drum signals."

I'm not a particularly brave person, and I try not to act foolishly around sick animals, but for some reason I took a risk, a dangerous chance. I stood up, my knees shaking, and stepped cautiously toward the cage on the wagon, carefully watching the back of Black Diamond.

My heart was pumping, a little tom-tom of excitement and fear. "I'm not going to poke you with a stick," I said, keeping my voice low and soothing.

The skin on her back rippled, the hairs spiking upward. She turned her head slowly to look at me. Her mouth opened slightly and her eyes narrowed. The white scar from the acid twisted the left side of her face downward in a grimace.

"Sorry," I said, and I knelt to the ground, signaling to her that I was a messenger come to her and I had to parley, to talk in her language, one of signs and movements. And I didn't feel like I was grovelling in terror in front of her, either. I felt humble and responsible to her for my mistakes and ignorance in not understanding her.

"Wraagh?" As I dropped down, the hair along her back seemed to soften, to lower.

"I apologize about the pickle," I said. "I should have warned you, but I wasn't thinking."

I tried to rise. She shifted a bit on her haunches, and the hair along her back popped up again. I bowed my head and waited, listening to her move on soft feet in her cage. After a while, I looked up. She faced me in the middle of her cage, staring at me, her head cocked to one side, curious but proud, a queen.

"Wraagh?" Her voice wasn't angry or shrill. It was questioning me, asking me in a puzzled way to show her what I meant by approaching her royalty in such a manner. What gifts would I offer instead of angry words, sticks and clubs?

I tried her language. "Wraagh."

She tilted her head downward and pursed her lips, showing her teeth, making a rasping sound. That's certainly not the right word, I thought, sinking down again.

I could get no closer to the cage that day without her rising, showing her teeth, threatening me. For the next few days, I approached her in the same way, humbling myself at one end of the trailer, arms over my head, on my knees, making myself familiar to her, a few more feet into her territory. Each day she allowed me to crawl a little closer to her. Although my breath caught in my throat and my heart raced, I ignored my fear and concentrated on learning her language, her body gestures and different voices.

41

Of course, I talked to her, also, telling her a little about my past, about how I dreamed of going to college someday, how I wanted a real family, what I thought of the circus and why I wanted to ride Colonel Bob's Deadwood stagecoach. Usually, she'd listen to me for a while, stare over my head as if she were surveying her domain, then quietly doze off, her great head resting on her chest, the swallows flitting in and out of the open doors.

Finally, on a Saturday afternoon, I was downtown eating at a long wooden counter. I was thinking about a picture of a wolf standing on a hillside in winter, overlooking a snowbound village, his breath a smoky signal of loneliness.

Passing me a salt shaker, a farmer who had given me corn told me the circus was playing about forty miles away and headed my way. "Betcha you're glad," he said. The sun had leathered his face and hands a dark brown.

I looked at the wolf picture. "I'm ready to get back to my village, all right." Once a person's lived under the Big Top, sawdust and animal smell and crowds mix in her blood. The circus is always there, a little village of warmth and light, someplace around the heart. I really missed my friends.

"You shore saved that big monkey," he said.

"Thanks. And thanks for the corn."

I had saved the circus's gorilla. I would present her to Colonel Bob and Jacko as if she were a traveller, an important guest from a strange land, and I were her guide.

But as I walked back toward the barn, across the brown Bermuda grass, I felt incomplete and hollow inside, like one of the brown cicada shells now petrified on the trunk of an elm tree. I knew I hadn't finished something.

Beyond the barn the weather waited, hot and still, like a caged animal, panting. Heavy thunderheads climbed upward in the west, tipped white, painted charcoal shading into blue-black on the bottom. Barn swallows darted, twittering, and a blue jay hopped across the grass beneath an elm, its dust-covered leaves hanging downward. The land needed rain.

"We did progress," I muttered to some sun-stained bleachers guarding the empty fairgrounds. I chewed on a sprig of Johnson grass, its head heavy with yellowing seeds, tasting of late summer. In a way I had journeyed in the barn farther than the circus had travelled to the next county.

I stepped inside the barn and around hay bales. "Okay," I said to Black Diamond. "Tomorrow it's Colonel Bob's Wild West and World's Greatest Menagerie."

"Naoom, naoom, naoom," she grunted softly at me as I crossed the barn.

"But it won't be all applause," I said. Too often circus life is hard, hard for everyone. "I know you'll do fine. You'll draw them to the menagerie, and I'll ride the stagecoach."

I picked up *White Fang*, the story about the dog in Alaska, and climbed up on the back of the wagon, slowly. Black Diamond didn't even look up from peeling an ear of corn.

"Still eating?" I settled down a safe distance from her cage. I was feeling good, thinking about how Jacko and I could talk again as we bumped along on the train, watching the smoke and hot cinders from the smokestack drift across the countryside. Soon I'd be safe in my village.

I opened my book to read the part where White Fang is chained up in a barn and men poke him with sticks to turn him into a fighting dog. I looked up from the page, and Black Diamond was squatting near her bars, her hands folded in her lap. Her posture reminded me of an old clown who had watched me as a child play with the costumes and trunks in Clown Alley before my mother disappeared.

"I'll bet you'd like to hug me, too," I said to Black Diamond, looking at her cupped hands. They were delicate but powerful, too.

"Wraagh?" She answered softly.

I thought of my narrow bunk in the clown car. "No, I won't sleep next to you."

"Wraagh?" She lifted one hand to her side, her sausage-like fingers scratching her ribs beneath her loose fur.

"Yes, you'll get more food, and I'll talk to Jacko about building you a larger cage. You'll do fine."

Outside, thunder growled in the distance, like some large animal muttering in quick barks, stalking prey, hungry.

Black Diamond was shivering, her shoulders shaking. The thunder came again, and her eyes widened, and she tightened her neck and head down into her shoulders, flinching like someone was hitting her. In her eyes I could see the farmer, his face red, swinging the axe handle at her, banging the wood against iron and yelling—all of man's abuse to animals.

"I'm not going any place. You're acting like a big baby.

43

Thunder won't hurt you. You're safe in here. The storm will miss us again."

I was right. The thunder animal slunk away, leaving a black spoor on the horizon, muttering, eating the land up with hail and lightning someplace else, but the yellowish-green light outside the barn made me feel like I floated in a big wooden boat, bobbing in a sea of green mist, waiting for something to rush over me. Black Diamond and I sat together, silently, listening to the storm edge away, going away to Colonel Bob's circus where the wind and rain would rattle the Big Top's canvas.

"Wraagh?" In the dark, Black Diamond looked like a great boulder, the bars metal crisscrosses of darkness.

"Still nervous? Well, I can't sleep in the cage with you," I said, walking across the wagon. I hopped down, found my sleeping bag, and shouldered it back to my spot and unrolled it on the wagon's floor. "I'll sleep on this end, thank you."

"Naoom," she said.

"Yeah, naoom," I replied, lying down, smelling her strong animal fear. I was a safe distance from her, but at least Black Diamond knew I was there.

I lay atop my sleeping bag and floated off to sleep, listening to the chirrup, chirrup, chirrup of a cricket and a wind stirring the limbs of elm and sycamore trees outside of the barn. Then, I was dreaming my crazy dream of twisted shadows moving around in front of the flickering light, reaching for me. The light danced through the shadows around me, and I wanted to reach out, to free myself and touch a shadow. I stretched out my arm, feeling the ends of my fingers wriggling forward, my heart beating excitedly.

Kaboom, Kaboom. Boom. Oom. Naoom. Naoom. Kaboom.

Light flashed, whitewashing the hay bales, harnesses, and the metal tongue of the trailer at my feet, an arrow of flame plunging toward the hay bales. I curled myself into a tight ball, waiting for the thunder clap.

Kabo-oo-om. The blast rattled the barn, shaking its boards like an angry mule lunging, striking out against the walls. Lightning struck again, nearby, with another sizzling pop, cracking and tearing and splitting something. The mule kicked again in a bang of thunder, and then it was inside the barn, its heavy hooves pounding on the wagon, snorting in fear, struggling to escape.

Nearby a voice was crying, short whimpers of fear, like a child defeated and alone in the dark.

44

I looked up, now awake, and nearly screamed in fear. Somehow in my sleep, I'd turned around and rolled closer to Black Diamond's cage. I lay a few feet away, my feet nearly touching the bars, my head tilted back, eyes staring at Black Diamond, a shadow pressed against the bars.

Lightning sparked again, farther away this time, and Black Diamond quivered, her shoulders shaking in fear. Again another bolt struck, and my body froze, numb, unable to move.

Kaboom. Boom. Noom. Kaboom. The sounds deafened me.

She whimpered again. Black Diamond stretched her arm between the bars, reaching toward me. She could easily grab me, snatch me by my legs, and crush me against the bars, but she twisted her arm toward my hand, her hand extended, her four fingers up, shaking.

I reached out and touched the tips of her fingers, my fingers shaking. Her fingers were cool and soft like velvet. She didn't grab my hand. She cupped her fingers around the tips of my fingers, and her soft whimpering stopped, died away as we listened to the wind howl in from the north, another predator stalking and chasing the thunder mule away to the south.

A Whack on the Head

Colonel Bob's Incredible Circus, Menagerie and Wild West Show—The Greatest Train and Wagon Show in the World—rolled into town the next afternoon.

His long, white hair tied up beneath a black, cowboy hat, Colonel Bob strutted into the barn with Jacko. "Is the money-maker still alive?" he asked, his eyes running over me. He jumped up on the bed of the wagon, grabbed a long rake handle, and rattled it through the bars.

Black Diamond jumped out of her corner, where she was peeling a banana; rushed toward the bars, growling, and thumped her chest; and then slammed the water bucket against the floor, spraying water through the bars.

"Nasty temper. The way I like'em. Brings in the crowds—and more money." The Colonel laughed and tugged at his goatee. He jumped up and down, squatted like Black Diamond, and beat his chest.

Black Diamond screamed with rage. "Aargh!"

"Ride 'em cowboy. Whoopee ki-yeah! That's a good, strong cage, he's in."

Jacko stared at me, and his eyes narrowed, a muscle twitching like a taut wire in his black face.

"That's a she, sir," I said. I was furious, but I bit off what I started to say, what I really wanted to say, about how I felt.

"Whatever. You're the boy who watched her. You did a great job. I appreciate it. What were you doing before?" He lifted white eyebrows toward the brim of his cowboy hat.

"She's in the Clown Alley," Jacko said. "But I could use Samathana to help me—"

"Nope, we're always short on clowns. Load that big baboon up and let's go. Gotta be there by nightfall," Colonel Bob said. He spun on his boot heels as if he were going to draw his pistol and pop a flashing silver dollar out of the sky.

I didn't climb up with the joeys but rode with Jacko on the snake wagon. I was so mad that I couldn't talk for two hours. Jacko knew it, so he didn't say anything. We sat in silence, rolling along under a sky washed blue from the rain, past fields of ripening, crimson milo, listening to the wood creak and smelling the sweating horses.

Behind us, at the end of the line of wagons, Black Diamond roared in anger at me, a howl of frustration. Her voice was pitiful. Jacko glanced toward the end of the line and then at me, waiting for me to say something.

"You did a good job with her," Jacko said, breaking into my silence. "You'd make a good animal person helping me out in the menagerie, so don't you blow this two-bit circus."

"I'm a joey again. Colonel Bob changes me around like a worn-out costume."

"I'll talk to him."

I thought about that for a mile or so of wind-stunted hedge rows, their tops leaning to the south. "No, I won't run off," I said. "I love the circus too much, I guess. Most of the time."

But I felt like that wolf in the picture overlooking the village. It's funny: sometimes a person wants to live inside the village, comfortable and warm, but at other times she wants to live away from it because it's too narrow, too confining.

Jacko's voice sounded relieved. "It's kind of like life." He rubbed his hand through gray whisker stubble. "It's rough at times and it doesn't go down all easy like that pink cotton candy."

"I wanted to move up. Get in the finale," I said.

"Maybe you will. Don't stop dreaming because of a little upset. Keep working on it," he said.

Jacko was right. I could still show Colonel Bob I deserved a spot atop the Deadwood stagecoach. I'd create a gag, a blow-off so funny that the audience and Colonel Bob would die of laughter. I'd burn the tent down around them. Sure, I hadn't liked the way Colonel Bob had treated Black Diamond, and I was still mad because he hadn't thanked me for staying in the barn with her. Yet progress takes a lot of work, and it isn't always easy. I'd expected too much, imagined that the Colonel would reward me with a job in the finale for tending Black Diamond. Didn't everyone in the circus do odd jobs—help drive tent pegs, pull wagons out of the mud, pack a sick person's gear? Everybody needed to cooperate in this village. I'd wanted an instant promotion for performing an odd job for the good of the circus.

I tried to understand my feelings by returning to the idea about working for the whole and not being so selfish, mulling it over like a horse chomping some worn-down and overgrazed pasture. Eventually, I gave up, but I was dissatisfied with the way Colonel Bob had treated me, barely thanking me for saving his investment. And I hadn't forgotten the way he had shaken the rake handle at Black Diamond. I admired him, yet his callousness toward Black Diamond worried me for her.

"Jacko?"

"Yup?"

"You won't let anything happen to Black Diamond?"

"No. Don't worry about her, honey. You help me build a cage for her—a real cage. A large cage, so she won't be so stooped and cramped."

"Sure."

"Okay," Jacko replied. "We'll start building tomorrow afternoon after the opening performance."

The next afternoon in Garden City, Kansas, I was standing in the back entrance to the Big Top, watching George the Magnificent guide his liberty horses around the ring, making them spin, dance, stand up on their hind feet, by a flick of his head or a soft spoken command.

Behind me, Jacko had lined up his cat wagon, waiting to pull Old Satan the African Killer into the ring. Colonel Bob couldn't afford a real animal trainer, so Jacko became Sultan the Barbarian. He pranced around the ring, shouting some mumbo-jumbo, dressed in a leopard skin and a tall black hat, acting as if he were an African king. As the drums rattled, he'd kneel and wave his whip at Satan, who usually was yawning in his cage, bored with all of the hullabaloo and trying not to fall asleep. Then Jacko always would pretend that he was going to open Satan's cage door, bring him out, and wrestle the African Killer.

Just as he had worked the audience's fears up, a few of the other joeys and I, dressed up like animals, would rush in, confuse his routine, and Old Satan would stay in his cage. The audience would laugh at the clowns, forget about the lion, and imagine they'd seen a real animal act.

That day I was a gorilla, in a dusty, black costume with cardboard feet and a rubber chest, still holding one of my big rubber gag hammers. A yellow tabby cat with a painted face, rope whiskers, and large cardboard ears covered with yellow felt stood next to me. We were talking and laughing about a couple of kids smearing ice cream on their faces.

I heard a low growl like a saw cutting wood behind me and shuffled my cardboard feet around, slowly. Old Satan was crouched outside his cage, his ears pulled back and his tail swinging back and forth, his belly quivering above the ground.

"What's the commoti—," the joey beside me said. He looked at Old Satan, gasped, scrambled backward, ran.

Old Satan snarled again, lifting his lips to show two yellow, worn teeth, and plopped his belly to the ground. I felt pounded into the ground like a tent stake stuck in the mud, my heart booming in my chest and my breath coming in short gasps.

Behind me the bugles and trombones squeaked and squealed into a ragged version of "Shoo Fly, Don't Bother Me." The song, a musical Western Union, had warned all the circus hands that an animal was loose.

Then, Old Satan snuggled down closer to the ground, the way house cats do when they're stalking a bird in the grass, and bellied along toward me, his black tail tuft twitching in little, tight circles of danger.

"Hey, there, Old Satan." Jacko and Edward the Sword Swallower popped out from behind Satan's wagon with a cord net stretched between them.

The lion glanced over his shoulder, growled, his shoulder muscles rippling, lowering himself, trying to decide which way to go. I was still a lonely tent peg, anchored only to the sky, feeling like the circus had pulled up stakes and left me behind.

Behind me the kids squealed and laughed at something in the ring. Old Satan hunkered down even more. Suddenly, he lunged forward, down the canvas funnel toward me, his tail rotating like a brown windmill.

"Hey, it's not your turn." I uprooted my feet and stepped forward, yelling.

At the sound of my voice, the lion skidded in the dirt and stopped in front of me, about four feet away, glaring.

He snarled. As his shoulder flinched, I bonged him on the nose with the rubber head of the long hammer.

"Yeow," he screamed, lunging at me. His claws ripped through the front of my monkey suit, snipping monkey fur like a giant scissors.

I stumbled back, hammer raised, ready to whack him again, but he ran—backwards into Jacko's net, a brown ball of anger, biting and clawing, rolling himself up in the cords, caught.

Later, outside the tent, I stood in a circle of people, watching them lift an exhausted Satan back in his cage. I tried to drink a cup of water, but my hand was shaking so badly that I kept slopping water down the front of my monkey suit.

"Good job, Sammy," Edward the Sword Swallower said, nodding toward me as he snapped the cage lock.

"Good thing you were dressed for the occasion, honey." Jacko pointed to my suit, his face looking sick. His tired voice leaked tension, like air escaping from a balloon.

I looked down at the front of my gorilla costume. Chunks of rubber chest and fur dangled where Old Satan had clawed the suit. Beneath the shreds, I could see that Old Satan's swipe had left one red welt across the top of my stomach, but his claws hadn't broken my skin.

Jacko was going to hug me, I think, when Colonel Bob walked up to Old Satan's cage and shook the lock.

"That cat cost me two hundred dollars five years ago," he said. He stroked his beard into a white point and looked around, accusingly. "Who let him out?"

"An accident. The lock jiggled loose," Jacko said.

"Don't let it happen again. I can't afford to have a cat loose in a Kansas cornfield. Bad publicity and it'd cut into my profits. Where's the joey who stopped him?"

I lifted one rubber hand.

Colonel Bob's eyes snaked over me, up and down, like he was judging an animal that he was considering buying. His looks made me feel uneasy, as if I were but a piece of his property. I looked away. I knew he didn't recognize me in my gorilla costume.

"What's your name?" He pointed a half-chewed cigar, wet, tooth marks on one end, at me.

"Sammy Starr," I said. "I'm the same person that—"

"I know," he said. "Mr. Starr, see me in my wagon in half an hour." Colonel Bob wheeled around and people stepped out of his way.

"That's Saman . . . ," Jacko muttered. He walked up to an empty water pail and kicked it into the spokes of a wagon wheel.

A New Idea

A half hour later, I stood outside Colonel Bob's red wagon, staring at it, still mad, rehearsing what I would and would not say to him if he fired me for facing Old Satan.

White letters two feet high announcing Colonel Bob's Incredible Circus, Menagerie, and Wild West Show—The Greatest Train and Wagon Show in the World marched down the wagon's side, past the head of a golden giraffe and a hippo with red mouth and foot-high teeth, into a freshly painted, snarling gorilla face. Black Diamond had never looked so mean, I thought, as I climbed the wooden steps to the Colonel's door and rapped an iron door knocker shaped like an elephant.

Colonel Bob barked for me to come in, and I opened the door and stepped inside the wagon. In the back, he was writing on a small roll-top desk, its cubbyholes and slots filled with papers and letters, black ledger books and dime novels. On one novel's cover, a big game hunter in cowboy boots, a dagger, and white hat faced a lion, a rhinoceros, and a bull elephant.

He glanced up and nodded at me with a quick jerk of his head and said, "Just a minute." He dipped a gold fountain pen into an ink bottle, sucked up some ink, and chicken-scratched some more, blotted the letter with blue paper, folded the letter in an envelope, and finally slowly turned toward me.

"Standing up to that lion was bold," Colonel Bob said, motioning for me to come closer to him. "I couldn't have done better myself. Bully for you!"

"Old Satan was just scared," I said. "He was looking for a way out. I didn't even think."

"You didn't run, though, and that's courage. You probably saved the lives of two, maybe three children. Look at these mementos—when I didn't run." Before him, he waved long white fingers covered with rings.

The walls of his wagon were covered with animal skins and heads and framed photographs of men clutching rifles, posed, stiff as mannequins, in front of dead elephants and dead buffaloes and dead tigers and dead lions.

"I was a crack shot. Still am. Got that lion in one shot in the Serengeti. He was just getting ready to eat his dinner." He pointed to a tan hide, ragged moth holes speckling it.

"Drilled that rhino from four hundred yards. He threatened us and was walking away, so it was a tough head shot." Light reflected off the rhino's horn and glassy eyes, frozen ice against the dark wood of the wall.

"The monkey was a challenge, too. That devil stood up and shook his fists at me. I don't talk that way, I'll tell you." Standing up, he turned me toward a corner. There a gorilla head stared out, mounted on a board, his mouth stretched back to show his teeth, his eyes dull black, like chunks of coal, not diamonds.

Don't think about it, I thought, but I couldn't stop my imagination. I kept thinking of Black Diamond's face, the way she'd looked at me in the barn as I dripped water from the hose into her mouth. And then her face would float over the features of the mounted head and become the dead gorilla. The gorilla head turned my stomach. I shut my eyes to block out the idea.

Across my shoulders, I could feel what I call my upset muscle twitch. I started to compliment the Colonel on his hunting ability—in my driest manner—and to excuse myself, but I didn't speak. I still wanted to star in the finale, to feel the audience's eyes fixed on me. I was willing then to compromise a lot for progress, to satisfy my ambition.

The Colonel was still talking, rambling on about his shooting exploits, but I wasn't listening to him very carefully until he mentioned progress. "So that's progress, you see. The taming of the animals, of the wilderness, the bringing of civilization to nature's dark areas. Like you faced down the lion," he said. He crossed his arms across his white, silk shirt with *BT* monogrammed in blue stitching above a pocket and cocked his head on his shoulders, satisfied with himself, a slick preacher beaming self-confidence from his pulpit over his congregation.

"I want you to work with the animals. Help Jacko."

I saw my stagecoach bouncing off in a whirl of dust and leaving me in my clown outfit, upset. "With the animals?" The question caught in my throat.

"Yup. Colonel Bob's Incredible Circus, Menagerie, and Wild West Show—The Greatest Train and Wagon Show in the World. You've shown you have a real knack for God's critters. Nursing that gorilla and now backing down the lion."

"But I—"

He waved his hands in front of his face, a satisfied smile plastered around the cigar. "No, no. No need to thank me. I know you're pleased that you're making progress. It's an important job. I need you to work with those animals. And I have plans for that monkey. He'll bring us in a lot of money. A real old-fashioned gold mine."

"What plans?" I asked, suspiciously.

"I'm planning on seeing The Wizard someday."

"Wizard?"

He narrowed his eyes at me in disbelief. "Edison. Thomas Edison. Surely you've heard of The Wizard of Menlo Park. Yup! My show in Menlo Park with The Wizard. Imagine that! Light bulbs! It's all coming, I tell you, and I'll be part of it. My Living Tableau under light bulbs!" Smiling, he spread his arms as if a crowd were clapping for him in the center ring.

"A table?"

"You bet. We'll make that monkey part of America's Living Tableau." The Colonel shook his head, smiled, and twirled one end of his white mustache between his thumb and forefinger like he was rolling a cigarette. He was enjoying my confusion.

"How can—"

"No, not that kind of table. A tableau. All the big circuses have them. They use them in the parades. Fancy, carved wagons—with dragons, gods, goddesses, gold trim, the works to illustrate some idea about America."

I knew what magic word he was going to toss out next, to weave into his little sermon.

He looked enraptured. "Progress, my young lady. My tableau will display America's progress from the depths of the savage until the land blossomed into the fruit of technology and civilization, the promised land of redemption. The Land of Canaan. Progress, I say." Colonel Bob pressed his hand over his heart and tilted his head back when he finished, lifting his pointed chin and looking down his nose with half-closed eyes, as if he were waiting for a murmur of amens. Outside one of the mules brayed, a loud snort, flattening in a trumpet-like squeal. The Colonel acted like he didn't hear the noise, but his eyebrows arched.

"And I need you to help achieve my . . . er, all our dreams."

"But I really—"

"Don't thank me, now. You'll get a dime a week raise. Besides, clowns are men, not girls. People figure out there's a girl behind that clown outfit and they'll complain. Why just the other day I had some official prowling around here, looking for runaways. Said he was from an orphanage." He arched his eyebrows to make sure I understood his threat.

I did. "I understand."

The Colonel didn't even blink an eye. "Good. I appreciate your wanting to help me, er, us progress, but that menagerie will keep you plenty busy while we build the tableau. We'll start with the tableau in Dodge City," Colonel Bob said as I started out the door. "You'll want to tag along with Jacko then."

Dodge City? Why did the Colonel want to begin in Dodge City? I didn't ask him. He was the manager, could see all of his show's parts, owned the circus, and we worked together for him. He did everything—paid the bills, scheduled the trains, fed the animals, checked the tents, directed the show, opened and closed the gates, and counted the money.

As I crossed the lot to talk to Jacko and to see Black Diamond, I stopped in front of the menagerie tent beside the ticket booth, a blue box. The tent's yellow-and-black-striped top wiggled like a caterpillar in the breeze. A huge sign with red and black letters on a white background across the entrance announced the dangers inside the tent:

WILD BEASTS.
THRILLING. EXOTIC LIONS. BEARS.
5 CENTS.

A new sign beside the booth read:

SEE THE BLACK DIAMOND,
KING OF THE JUNGLE FROM DARKEST
AFRICA—A LIVE GORILLA.
AMAZEING. COLLOSSAL.
A MANEATER. DANGEROUS. 10 CENTS

At least Colonel Bob remembered her name, I thought. "Okay," I muttered. "Samantha, hold your temper and your tongue. Sure he's bulling you, but you don't want any free trips to the Sunnydale Orphanage for Wayward Girls. The Colonel knows the circus."

I thought to myself: If he wants to build a tableau wagon, he'll build one. There's a place on that tableau wagon for me. The wagon will turn into a spectacle better than the stagecoach, and I'll drive it, dressed in blue sequins, waving to people who really do appreciate me. By the time I stepped through the entrance to the menagerie, I was—if not satisfied with myself—excited and happy at my good fortune, driving Colonel Bob's Living Tableau at the head of the largest parade in history, headed for Bridgeport.

Building a Cage

Inside the menagerie tent, on the top of an extra-long wagon, Jacko was pounding away at Black Diamond's new cage, nailing pine boards to some railroad ties coated with sharp-smelling creosote. Old Satan was sleeping in his cage, breathing in short wheezes, his paw and tail drooping down. And Black Diamond sat in the corner of her cage, watching Jacko bang away with his hammer. When she saw me, she stirred a little on her haunches, unfolded her hands, and grunted a little, a low cough.

I stopped in front of her wagon, dropped on my hands and knees and inchwormed toward her wagon and then crawled up on it, keeping my eyes down. I waited, my legs trembling, wondering what she'd do.

Black Diamond stirred and moved toward the bars. "Wraagh?"

I crawled a little forward and glanced up. Black Diamond was watching me, her head tilted to one side. She looked thin, her fur now dull, and the corners of her eyes were crusted over with dust and eye discharge.

I clucked to her in a low voice, trying to remember how we'd talked in the barn. "I'm glad to see you again," I said softly. I didn't mention the mounted heads I'd seen in Colonel Bob's trailer.

After a few moments, I crawled away, Black Diamond went back to her corner, and I jumped off the wagon.

"You see that?" Jacko asked.

"What?" I asked, brushing straw off the knees of my jeans.

"She grabbed the head of lettuce on her way back." Jacko scratched at his beard. "I was worried about her appetite. She's glad to see you."

"She—for one—listens to me. I'm supposed to work with you." I pushed my hands in my pockets and glanced around at the cages.

"Well, don't act so excited," Jacko said, snapping at me. He looked at me disgustedly.

"I wanted . . . " I felt like crying.

"Child, that's a circus for you. Like life, I guess." I felt like walking away, leaving, blowing the outfit, but he reached out and touched my shoulder with his big hand with square fingernails. "I didn't mean to sound so harsh. I'm sorry."

"I know," I said. "I just wanted to move up . . . to progress." Now, the word sounded like a piece of tin rattling in the wind.

"Well, as long as you're here," he said, motioning toward Black Diamond, "then that ape and me are progressing, I reckon. Grab that hammer."

We worked the rest of the afternoon, hammering scrap lumber to the railroad ties, twisting heavy screws and bolts into the wagon, fitting iron bars to wooden slots. Black Diamond watched us for a while as if she understood what we were building and then rolled over and went to sleep, her breathing lifting her fur gently and evenly.

Finally, we stopped. Sweat beaded across Jacko's forehead. He wiped his neck and face with a blue bandanna, breathing heavily. I leaned against a corner post, my legs stretched out in front of me, my arms heavy from swinging the hammer, hands aching. My white ankles stuck out between the tops of my heavy shoes and white socks and the bottom of my frayed jeans. I was growing again that summer, shooting upward, and sometimes I stumbled on my long legs.

I glanced up. "A large cage."

Jacko laughed. "Yup. Put some paint, cardboard, designs over the top, and presto, circus magic-Colonel Bob's new dream."

"A tableau?"

"*The* tableau," he said. "He's gonna call it The Vision of America."

"With Black Diamond?" I couldn't yet imagine what Colonel Bob intended to do with his tableau.

Jacko shook his head, smiling, as if enjoying a private joke. "But not just Black Diamond. She's only part of the display. Dodge City, here we come." His gold tooth flashed.

"Dodge City?" I waited for him to continue. What else would Colonel Bob add to a tableau featuring a caged gorilla?

"We're going to find Little Wolf in Dodge City." He held his arms before his chest, fingers outspread, and shrugged his shoulders upwards.

We had all worked too long in the hot Kansas sun, I thought. "A little wolf?"

"No, an Indian named Little Wolf." Jacko rose, his hands pushing against his knees, and lifted himself up, making his joints pop. He started gathering hammers, nails, saws. "You betcha. Colonel Bob wants a tableau with a gorilla and an Indian, so we'll give him one, pronto." His voice sounded sarcastic. "Too much of that Barnum fella, if you ask me."

Jacko was right, of course. We'd never become that famous and show Feejee the Mermaid, George Washington's nurse. "How long until we finish the cage?" I asked him, as he clanked the tools into a scarred, green toolbox, making Black Diamond stir uneasily in her sleep.

"By next week."

"Do me a favor?" I asked. I smiled my best smile, the one that curls my mouth up on the left side and makes my dimples show.

"What, Sammy?" Jacko raised heavy eyebrows doubtfully, puckered his lips, and tugged at a heavy earlobe.

I nodded toward Black Diamond. "She needs exercise. Something to do. She's nothing but a prisoner in a cage. Remember, you said you'd build something for her to do inside her cage." How could he have forgotten?

"I dunno about . . . like what?"

"Anything? A swing. Maybe a puzzle. For her imagination."

Jacko drooped the corners of his mouth downward in thought as he fumbled for, found, and tugged a half-chewed cigar out of a sawdust-and-sweat-stained pocket. "She's got an imagination?" His eyes locked on mine, as if to say Samantha Starr was blessed with the imagination and it wasn't always a blessing.

"Why wouldn't she?" I asked.

Jacko looked at Black Diamond's back. "It's a pretty sleepy imagination."

"Boredom. Like an old person with nothing to do."

"Colonel Bob wants the tableau a certain way and I don't have time to chase down tires, fix puzzles . . . " He sounded serious, too serious, I thought, suspiciously.

"Then, I'll do it," I said, stretching my tired back muscles, standing up. "You can forget you ever mentioned it." I felt hurt that he'd forgotten his promise.

"Well . . . maybe we could . . . " He shook his head, his face quizzical, and snapped the toolbox lid shut.

"Please," I said, tugging at his shirtsleeve.

He turned slowly and smiled, flashing his gold tooth, a big smile of satisfied victory. I wanted to slap him and hug him at the same time. "At last. A *please*. Okay, Samantha. It's nice to see you thinking about someone other than yourself. Not cage yourself away all of the time."

Sure I had acted selfishly, but a person can't depend upon others too much. People die, circuses move on. Too much caring can be a snare too. I'd never risk too much of myself for Jacko, Joey, and Colonel Bob. Even though we were odd, different, in our circus, we weren't always family, and probably never would be.

We fed and watered the animals that afternoon. As we worked under the canvas, carrying buckets of water, cleaning cages, Jacko didn't say much, only showed me a few things and introduced me to the feeding routine. I listened, but mostly, I wondered about animal imagination and started to design the inside of Black Diamond's cage, completing it with wheels and boxes and swings.

Little Wolf

In Dodge City a week later, I wasn't prepared for the flat, immense prairie and blue sky like the inside of an umbrella.

Brown grasshoppers popped up from the ditches like hot kernels of corn inside Uncle Frankie's popcorn machine, and dust devils lifted themselves out of the ground in the distance, twirling their air capes and shaking their dust pitchforks. Heat mirages shimmered across wheat fields, melting greens and yellows and browns in watery smudges, flat streaks against the horizon.

I was bouncing in the back of the wagon over potholes in a pitted dirt road, listening to Colonel Bob and Jacko talk about Little Wolf. Colonel Bob was rambling on about his long friendship with Little Wolf. What the Colonel said about himself and Little Wolf sounded like tall tales or Frank Reade dime novels. "A Lakota from Standing Rock. Best shot west of the Mississippi—next to me, of course," the Colonel said, snorting and shooting a tobacco stream toward the road. "Used to ride with him when I shot buffalo for the Great Northern in the Dakotas."

"In the 1880s?" Jacko asked, not really interested, as if he'd heard the yarn before.

The Colonel swiveled in the buckboard seat, especially so I could hear. He acted excited, telling his story. "No, in the late 60s, after the War. Killed a lot of them together. I saw him drop one a quarter of a mile a way with two shots in a heavy wind. He used the first slug to judge the wind speed, so he could see how the bullet moved."

Old frontiersmen often bragged about their shooting, and I remembered Colonel Bob said that he was even a better shot. He probably killed buffalo at two miles with a peashooter or elephants with circus batons.

But I was polite. "He's a crack shot then?" I asked. Why did Colonel Bob want him for his circus wagon? How would he use him in the parade?

"One of the best, I tell you. We toured Europe with Buffalo Bill and Annie Oakley. Made a bundle. He could have moved into Annie's place after she hurt herself in the train wreck."

"Why didn't he?" Jacko asked, now curious.

"Dadgum if I know," Colonel Bob said. He shrugged. "One day he up and vanished. Packed his bag and shipped back to America. He's been hiding out here since then. Wasting his talent and not progressing. Drinking, I heard. Feeling sorry for hisself. Just like an Injun."

Ahead I could see a small dot with light around it on a hill, one of those wind-sanded bumps that magically jump out of the sun and sky and grass, like an animal grazing alone. I knew it was strange—riding in the back of a dusty buckboard, under a flat Kansas sky—but goose bumps walked up and down my suntanned arms and I could almost hear something, see something just beyond my sight, like an animal loping beside the wagon.

As we came closer, the dot formed into a house, a red three-story Victorian house with an eight-sided tower in the front, reflecting sunlight and the prairie from its windows, like a gigantic mirror. The tower's roof ended in a spiral of iron, sharp, a lance higher than the two brick chimneys on the slate roof.

As Colonel Bob hitched the horse's reins through a tarnished brass ring on the stone horse head, for an instant a large white dog appeared in a second-story window and watched us from behind the glass. I shivered in the heat, beneath my damp shirt, and glanced behind me, feeling as if something were watching my back. I can feel animals that way, sense them observing me just out of my sight. But nothing stood behind me, except broom grass melting into blue sky and a line of low-slung hills like distant linked elephants marching on the horizon. When I turned around, the dog had disappeared.

The front door, its woodwork carved sunflowers and lightning bolts, opened, and Little Wolf stepped out onto the porch. A tall man dressed in jeans, moccasins, and blue work shirt, he watched us silently as we walked toward him, single-file on a sunken brick sidewalk between white horns, bleached animal skulls, and a line of chalk vertebrae like small lizards hiding in the dried grass.

"Little Wolf. It's me," Colonel Bob said, his voice uncertain, lifting his hand in salute, as if he were a traveling salesman calling on a reluctant customer.

As the porch steps creaked under our feet, Little Wolf didn't say anything and didn't move, strong hands dangling at his sides, watching us, as if he were trying to decide whether to vanish through the door or brush us away as if he were knocking away dusty tumbleweeds.

"Hi, Chief. You remember me? It's Colonel Bob Thackerby." The Colonel took off his white hat and sponged away the ring of sweat on his forehead with a white handkerchief.

Little Wolf nodded his head slowly and stepped back inside the door, bars of light in his eyes caging me for a minute, holding me in their gaze.

"Come in." He led us into the tower room. Through the windows, the sunlight melted into the room like hot amber, flowing over plants and flowers, violets, roses, some cacti, in blue and red bottles.

Colonel Bob didn't waste any time in reminiscing. "I want you to come back and work with me in my Wild West show," he said.

"Those days are gone," Little Wolf said. His wind-and-sun-weathered face was narrow, with high cheek bones, a long nose cutting downward like a quick hatchet stroke. A line of blue beads and small white stones circled his neck.

"Of course. Of course, I understand that," the Colonel said. "But we need to remember them through the Wild West show."

Little Wolf's eyes flashed and he shook his head. "Why? No, the shows lie."

Colonel Bob cupped his chin in his hand and looked down at a faded carpet, tracing with the square toe of his dusty boot a rose. "You had a bad time with Buffalo Bill Cody, I know, but my show is different. More authentic."

Little Wolf's long fingers brushed through his shoulder-length, iron-gray hair. He stared at me, his dark eyes holding me, studying me carefully. I tried to avoid his eyes, but I couldn't turn my face away. I felt flushed and my heart pounded. My breath tightened, caught in my chest as if a force were squeezing me. His eyes reminded me of Old Satan's eyes, deep and mysterious and dangerous, calculating, waiting. "She works with animals?" He tilted his head toward me.

How did he know? I wondered.

"Yes, she's our lion tamer." Colonel Bob laughed. He told Little Wolf how I'd conked Old Satan on the head and how he and Jacko had trapped him in the net.

It was an odd situation. Little Wolf's eyebrows lifted and he stared at me, netting me between the bars of light and his black pupils. Then the light in the room changed, becoming more indistinct, blurred, the reds and yellows and blues blending, swirling together into a kaleidoscope of colors. Samantha, you've been sitting in the sun too long, I thought, knowing that wasn't what was happening.

At first, I felt embarrassed, uncomfortable, yet wanting to come closer to him, as if I were a wolf circling a campfire, as if Little Wolf were searching inside my heart. Then I relaxed and dropped down the cage doors to my heart. I wondered if he liked what he saw, but I didn't particularly care if he disapproved.

Colonel Bob's voice interrupted my thoughts. "It'll be different this time. I want you to help show the glory of the Indians. No more riding and robbing stagecoaches. No more savage Indians."

Little Wolf shook his head, the corner of his mouth pulling down. "No."

Colonel Bob's shoulders sagged a bit. He walked across the room and looked out the windows, cupping his hands behind his back. He rocked in his boots, leather creaking on the oak floor. Then he swung around and faced Jacko, Little Wolf, and me.

"You're right. You've good reasons not to go with me, and I don't blame you," he said, pausing after each sentence as if he were preparing for a hunting expedition. "Those old Wild West outfits show history wrong, make the Indians look silly, like savages, savages from Africa or some other place. I'm not asking you to do that again. But, I need you to ride on a fancy parade wagon that'll show progress, how America has changed. For the better. We're going to progress, but we need to remember the

Indians. My show'll keep your story alive. Little Wolf, I know you were a better shot than Annie Oakley. I know why you left Buffalo Bill. He wouldn't let you shoot because you were an Indian. It was unfair. You were the best."

The Colonel paused, and he swung his hand around the room. "You're getting older." He tapped his chest. "We all are. You'll need some money for old age, to help keep up your place. I need a crack shot act, and I'm only asking you for this summer. I promise you'll be back by fall. What do you say?"

Little Wolf didn't say a word. In the silence, the wind whipped against the side of the house, surging around windows like water, trying to float the old houseboat across the land on a sea of wind and grass.

Didn't the Colonel understand that nothing would make Little Wolf come with us? And I didn't care how well he shot, Colonel Bob's speech made me uncomfortable, and probably embarrassed Little Wolf.

"Remember that last buffalo hunt? On the Yellowstone?" Colonel Bob asked suddenly, almost pleading now. "I don't want to mention it, but I helped you when you needed me, so don't make me beg."

Little Wolf stared at the Colonel, and then he nodded his head, his jaw tightened. "I remember," he said. "That was long ago when we killed too much."

Colonel Bob's face lit up. "That we did."

Little Wolf thought awhile and then said, "But you saved my life. We are getting old. Men should repay their debts while they can." He paused, considering, his face quiet, and glanced at me. Now his eyes were dark stones, flecked with slivers of quartz. "Yes, I'll go with you, but just for this summer."

Jacko and I sat on the front steps, not saying anything as we waited for Little Wolf to pack. Colonel Bob planted himself in the sidewalk and chucked pebbles at the animal skulls, laughing whenever a stone bounced off one, looking like a kid waiting on his parents to finish their shopping. In about an hour, Little Wolf came out of the house, locked the door behind him and dragged a trunk to the wagon, his rifle in a fringed scabbard, slung over one shoulder. I was glad to leave, to head back to the circus.

On the way back to town, Little Wolf rode in the back of the wagon, a black derby on his head, his wooden trunk beside him, plastered over with old steamboat tickets. He didn't say anything to me, but he made me uneasy with his watching, his silence as he watched his house shrivel on the horizon. Once he turned and stared at me, his eyes uneasy, and I thought of an old wolf, wounded, back legs shaky, alone and watching a group of approaching hunters, still proud, reserving his strength. I wondered what he saw waiting for him in my village, our mudshow.

A Rich Plan

The next week, the Kansas countryside looked the same as we chugged east toward Missouri, smoke from the engine hazing the wheat stubble and patches of green woods along sluggish, brown creeks. We steamed through towns strung along the railroad tracks, and sometimes we'd stop at the larger ones, the ones with a main street of small businesses fronting the tracks, and put on a show for a few days before moving on.

The train engineer would grind our circus train onto a side track in the railroad yards. We'd unload the wagons from the cars, hitch up the horses and set up on vacant lots or fairgrounds—places with space for the tents and water for the animals. I'd do whatever Jacko asked me to do-pulling canvas, driving stakes, unloading, carrying water, moving boxes, feeding, guarding the animals.

Black Diamond kept her eye on me, and if I moved around in the tent, she'd scoot from one side of the cage to another, keeping as close to me as possible. Sometimes during performances, I'd bring Black Diamond the best fruit and vegetables I could find and sit close to her cage and listen to the band play, smelling her heavy animal odor, whistling and humming, explaining the show to her.

One Saturday evening, the crickets were humming, and the late summer air smelled moist and crisp, the way the year does in early autumn when elm leaves yellow and curl along the edges and blue jays and crows squawk high in sycamore trees, fretting about a fading summer.

Under the Big Top, Little Wolf was performing his final shooting tricks, breaking an egg by sighting his Henry rifle over his shoulder and by looking in a mirror. Black Diamond flinched at the crack of the rifle. She tucked her head down into her shoulders. "Wraagh?"

"Wraagh is about right," I said.

I flipped a red juggler's ball in the air. I'd been practicing tricks in the tent, fooling around when Jacko and I weren't working on the cage or taking care of the menagerie animals.

Out of the corner of my eye, I glimpsed Black Diamond push her hand upward, her fingers cupped and curling as if she were tossing a ball in the air, juggling.

I repeated her gesture, tossing an imaginary ball upward and catching it as it came down. "Wraagh."

She mimicked me, her eyes following my hand. "Wraagh."

I almost fell off the end of the wagon. "You're trying to talk to me." My voice was excited and loud. "Do this, then." I covered my eyes with my hand and peeked between my fingers.

Black Diamond didn't move. Her brown eyes stared into mine, and then she picked up a cabbage head and carefully picked off pieces, poking them into her mouth, her jaw slowly chewing. I acted like I was eating a cabbage, making the same movements as she did. She just looked at me, now bored at my acting.

"Sorry," I said, disappointed. "Looking for something, I guess. I thought you were trying to tell me something."

I started thinking again about how people and animals communicate and understand each other. I listened to the band play its last number and sat on the wagon in front of Black Diamond's cage, waiting for the end of the show.

"Wraagh?"

"I'll bet if you could talk, you could tell me a lot, couldn't you?" I asked. "About capture and cages, huh? I'd like to hear about it someday."

I was feeling lonely, wanting a friend, someone to talk to, so I wiggled my fingers at Black Diamond, the way a child does when he tries to say bye-bye. And Black Diamond lifted her hand and wiggled her thick fingers back.

Excited, I waved at her again. She didn't move. She just sat watching me, her eyes alert.

I wiggled my fingers again, and she barely wiggled the tips of her fingers, not lifting her hand from her lap. What is it? I thought. What am I missing? Why does she seem to know certain signs but not others?

Then, I felt stunned, sensing something before I thought it out. My heart beating, I reasoned out what I'd seen. If she made some signs, then someone had worked with her. And if she could still repeat them, then she could remember. Remembering meant learning. Learning meant thinking and understanding.

I stood up in front of her cage and said, "Come here." I pulled my hand toward my chest, like I was fanning a breath of air toward me.

"Sammy, what are you doing?" The voice behind the wagon startled me, and I turned around.

Jacko and Little Wolf, still cradling his rifle in his arm, stood watching me at the end of the wagon. I hadn't even heard them walk up.

"I'm, uh . . . "

Little Wolf nodded, a smile flickering across his face.

"She understands me," I blurted out. "Watch." I turned to Black Diamond and said, "Wraagh." I wiggled my fingers at her.

Black Diamond didn't "Wraagh" back, and didn't move her hands. She stared at Little Wolf, the bottom part of her scarred lip lifted up slightly. Nodding his head, Little Wolf turned and walked out of the tent.

"The rifle scares her," I said to Jacko.

Jacko thumbed his favorite pair of red suspenders, stretching them away from his chest, and tilted his head at me, eyes raised in question. "Why do you think the gorilla can understand you?" he asked, as if he were humoring a small child.

I explained how I tried to talk to Black Diamond, what had happened in the barn, how Black Diamond had tried to imitate my signs.

"I doubt it, Sammy," he said. "You were probably imagining it, working to feed her. I understand. Do it myself with Old Satan over there, when there's no one around to talk to."

"No, I wonder if someone trained her before the farmer bought her," I said. I was excited at the idea but frustrated that Jacko doubted that Black Diamond had talked to me. "Don't you understand? She already knows some things, a language of signs. But I don't know them. *I'm* the one that can't talk to her."

"I don't . . . wait just a minute. I'll be right back." He limped away, leaving me standing on the wagon, trying not to think other things about Black Diamond I'd kept away, caged up in the back of my mind.

"She probably does understand you," rang out just when I was thinking this idea. The voice startled me, and I jumped a little. I looked up and Little Wolf stood below me, without his rifle and still wearing his circus outfit, fringed, buckskin legging, a blanket draped over a white shirt, beads, and a single white feather with a red tip hanging near his face.

"How did you . . . " I stammered.

"You were right. The rifle was making her nervous," he said, "so I put it in my wagon." His smile stamped little crows-feet at the corners of his eyes and rounded his cheekbones.

"No. I mean how did you know what I was thinking, now? Sort of."

"How did you see some of me? At my house."

What did I know about him, I wondered, trying to understand, remembering the odd feeling of something beyond my vision I'd sensed at his house. Yet I couldn't exactly define or shape my sensation into understanding. My face must have looked blank, and I felt awkward, exposed, as if something were stalking me from a distance, just out of sight.

"You'll remember again. Look for it again. I was surprised then, when you sensed it so early, but," he looked at Black Diamond, "now I know why."

"I don't—"

A voice interrupted us. "Hey, look at this." Jacko was walking toward us, waving papers in his hand. "Good gate tonight, so Colonel Bob didn't mind."

Feeling relieved he was there, I hopped off the trailer.

"You were right," Jacko said, shuffling the papers in his hand. He pointed a thick forefinger to a blue paper. "Black Diamond was at the New York Zoological Institute."

I looked at a paper I'd missed when we skimmed them in the wagon. Across the top, typed above a dotted line were the words "Language Studies—1892."

"Jacko, she *did* study language," I said.

"School, huh. Well, I don't care what it says, she can't talk," Jacko said. He rubbed his chin, his silver ring and turquoise rasping chin stubble. "Wonder how long she was there?"

I read from the page. "Acquired from Belgian Congo. Year-old female. Program terminated 1895. Sold 1897 to Barnes Circus." I looked at Jacko and Little Wolf, excited now. "And the farmer picked her up from the sideshow."

"She's probably forgotten most of whatever kind of language she learned." Jacko sounded doubtful.

"But she's been trained. It'll come back. We could . . ."

Jacko stopped me by holding up a thick hand. "Hold on. We haven't got time. We're too busy as it is."

"I could try," I said. "After we're finished with her new cage. I could . . . "

"Well, I'm not opposed to—"

"Good idea. Good idea," Colonel Bob said suddenly behind us. He clapped his whip against his buckskin pants as he spoke, explaining each word with a pop of leather against leather. "I wondered why you wanted those papers. Heard you talking about training that monkey in the new cage. Just what I had in mind. Make her part of America's Living Tableau. She'll show our evolutionary forefathers." The Colonel laughed, arching his white eyebrows upwards, pleased with his own humor.

I noticed Black Diamond had moved to the back of her cage. I handed Black Diamond's papers back to him. Apparently, the Colonel hadn't heard all of the conversation, and I wasn't going to explain what he'd missed.

Colonel Bob patted Little Wolf on the shoulder. "Fine shooting out there, my friend. Reminded me of old times." He spread his arms widely, smiling and bowing at the waist, proud of himself. "The crowd loved it." He glanced at me. "And you thought I was fibbing about his marksmanship. No, siree, I was not."

Jacko ducked his shoulders and Little Wolf tensed beside me.

"When will the new wagon be ready?" Colonel Bob stepped over and rapped his whip handle against a railroad tie.

"A week," Jacko said. "Maybe less. Need to move Black Diamond in. Finish the top. Do some more painting."

"Finish up then," the Colonel said. "We'll be in Missouri by then, heading for St. Louis." He pronounced it "Louie," stretching out the word like he was unwinding his bullwhip. "And we'll need something new to excite the city crowds. No rube stuff for them, my boy—uh, girl." He patted me on the shoulder.

I wanted to push his hand off and say my name, but I just nodded, listening to his enthusiasm, his talk, still captured by his excitement and ideas.

He waved his hand over the unfinished wagon, as if he were a priest blessing it. "It'll be all about our progress from animals and the past and the skills of the American Indian and now technology. The March of Man Through History, we'll call it." His voice was pitching upward in excitement.

"Technology?" Jacko was snipping off the end of a new cigar with his black-handled Barlow knife, carefully trimming the point.

"The world's changing. They're building cars now. Dirigibles. The wireless. We're a little outdated. We need a wagon to show the new ideas. We've got everything here." He pointed with his whip. "The gorilla. The skill of the red man. Everything except technology. But I've some ideas about that."

"You do?"

Colonel Bob looked at me and lifted his eyebrows the way a poker player does when he plays his ace. "You remember Hirum Peabody?"

Jacko thought a second, looking puzzled, and shook his head. "Nope. Never heard of him."

"Sure you have. The Creator of Mechanical Colossuses and Wonders. Call him Harum Scarum back East. Knew Barnum. He used to design calliopes for the John Robinson Circus. Brilliant. Absolutely brilliant." Colonel Bob looked smug.

"Steam calliopes? They're too danger—" Jacko said.

The Colonel didn't even hear his worry. "New ideas are *always* misunderstood. Anyway, we're heading his way. Lives in Missouri. He's retired and wasting his talents. Designing new contraptions. Not progressing like he should. He owes me a favor—well, maybe not, but I can convince him." The edge of a gold tooth glimmered beneath the Colonel's smile, and he waved his whip over the wagon like a magician's wand. "Get that cage in place before we see old Hirum. Boy, then won't he slap the power to it. Shoot us right into the 20th century along with all of those other contraptions."

Maybe the Colonel's tableau wasn't so crazy and we'd progress too, making more money so our circus would grow larger and bring in more customers and make more money and grow still larger. A huge circus, stretching across the continent, filled with a complete zoo—elephants and dancing bears and hippopotamuses—grew in my mind, and I was busy harvesting the profits, ringing up the sales on my brass cash register.

Someday, Colonel Bob, Jacko, Little Wolf, Black Diamond, and I could travel east, stop and chat with Edison about his light bulbs and progress and then on to New York and Madison Square Garden. All of us would have a great future in Colonel Bob's Incredible Circus, Menagerie and Wild West Show—The Greatest Train and Wagon Show in the World. We'd go on tour and ship our circus to Europe, to England, to Scotland, to France. Even to Russia maybe.

In the parades, Black Diamond would fit in perfectly in the Living Tableau, The March of Man Through History. I'd open a special tent for her along the midway and show the crowds how we talked with signs, how she followed me with her head and eyes, how she howled with rage. No, I wouldn't do that, but I'd charge them a Barber quarter for a peek at us. Why, I might even let Joey roll me in his trick barrel again. Tomorrow, I'd start working with Black Diamond, understanding her more, talking with her, preparing her and me for a rich future filled with silver dollars and gold eagles.

A Train Wreck

A week later, Jacko, Little Wolf, and I were inside our wagon, atop the menagerie's long flatcar, playing checkers, the pieces rattling and shimmying on the board as the train boomed along through the late afternoon toward Spring River, Missouri.

Through the window, the land was a blur of mist-covered hills, covered with blackjack oak and white-barked sycamores along rocky streams. Red barns, plastered with signs advertising Red Man Chewing Tobacco and faded political posters of Woodrow Wilson, overlooked water-soaked, hilly pastures, horses and cows grazing against split-log fences, their backs darkened by rain.

I moved a red checker piece forward, hoping Jacko wouldn't see that I intended to trap him by sacrificing one of mine to gobble up a couple of his unprotected pieces. "Your move," I said, nonchalantly, taking a drink of coffee from my tin mug, proud of my trap. A flash of lightning streaked outside. On a top bunk bed Little Wolf looked up from his book.

"Heavy rain tonight," he said, his voice rising above the rumble of thunder.

"It's miserable, all right. At least we don't show till tomorrow," Jacko said. His hand hovered over the piece I wanted him to move. He hesitated, looked up and smiled at me, and took his hand away.

Another bolt of lightning jabbed across the hills, and the wind whipped rain against the window glass, forming little pools at the bottom of the pane. I was glad Black Diamond was safe and dry inside her new cage atop the tableau wagon.

Air brakes whooshing and squealing, the train bumped a little, shifting the checkers to the edge of their squares. Warm coffee sloshed over my hand.

"Coming down the hill," Jacko said. "Right on time. Considering the weather and all." He edged his black piece toward an open square, toward my trap, tapping his checker forward with a square fingernail and—

BOOM! WRUMP! WANG! SCREECH!

Suddenly, I hurtled out of my chair, sliding forward, checkerboard and pieces floating in the air between Jacko and me. The table flipped over on its top, its legs pointed to the ceiling. Then my shoulder slammed into the door, white lights speckled blackness, and I was gasping for breath, trying to swim up from some great, cold depth. My breath shook my body.

The wagon stopped moving. Jacko lay on his stomach, arms outstretched, facing me, a shocked look on his face, the table on top of him, one hand still clutching a checker.

"You hurt?" Little Wolf was clearing a path toward us, moving chairs and tables away.

"Uh-huh." I nodded my head. It felt enormous, like a huge watermelon bobbing in a metal washtub. I was dizzy. The room pitched and rolled as I tried to stand.

"We've hit something." Jacko shoved the table away from himself with his feet and stood up, swaying. Outside the train, voices yelled, and a horse neighed in pain. Jacko and Little Wolf stepped through the mess and wrenched open the jammed door. I followed them, still dizzy.

Warm drizzle cleared my thoughts as I stood on the railroad flat car. On my right, a line of empty boxcars was parked a few tracks away, red and yellow and green, their colors brightened by the rain, their open doors gaping like mouths. Ahead, a brick railroad depot squatted in the mist, a heavy building with pointed roofs, in the fading light its Spring Hill sign a white block against dark bricks.

Toward the front of the train, black feathers of smoke twirled into gray sky and plumed out at the top, suspended like a broken wing over the tracks and depot. Fire engine bells clanged and bonged in the distance. One of the circus hands sprinted toward the front of the train, carrying a shovel and a crowbar, banging them together as he ran. Someone in a yellow raincoat, with no shirt, his shoes clogged with mud, followed, slipping and yelling.

Old Satan yowled. Raccoons squalled and chattered angrily.

"We've hit another train," Jacko said. He turned. The animal wagons were still in place. The ropes and chains had kept their wheels locked between blocks of wood. Old Satan roared a bellow of anger.

"Thank God. The tie-downs made it. They're okay," he said. "Sammy, double-check'em to make sure." He pulled a heavy coil of rope from the wagon, climbed off the railroad car, and ran after the yellow raincoat, gravel crunching beneath his feet.

Little Wolf and I started checking the animal cages. Old Satan was sitting up in his wagon, looking irritable, licking his paw, rolling it in tight, nervous circles over his face, his ears slanted back. The raccoons were darting back and forth in their cage between food pans and water buckets, growling, chattering, chittering. Their hollow tree limb had splintered against the wall of their cage, snapping off branches.

"Like Little Wolf in his bunk bed." Little Wolf laughed, shaking his head.

But we stopped laughing when we came to Black Diamond's new wagon. The ropes lashing one end of the canvas over the top of the wagon were off, and the canvas was torn and hung in tatters away from the cage, flapping against wet wood. I helped Little Wolf roll back the canvas, afraid and knowing what I'd find.

Her new cage was empty, the door wrenched ajar, the heavy padlock on the floor of the cage in pieces, shattered, a thick piece of pipe lying beside it.

Little Wolf picked up the lock and pipe, turning them in his hand. "She made her own key," he said, his eyes widening, looking at the pipe. "How did she get this?"

"I gave it to her." I pointed at an old rubber tire, an egg crate, a rubber ball, a dented washtub. "Those too. For something to do. She was bored." I felt stupid. My face was hot and flushed, and I thought I was going to cry. I hadn't thought far enough ahead, and now she was loose, afraid, in the rain.

Little Wolf patted me on the shoulder. "Don't worry. We'll find her." He pulled off some rope from the canvas, walked to the edge of the flatcar, and climbed down. I followed him, trying to escape the question that followed me, spinning in my mind, around and around like a small dark tornado, twisting me into knots of misery.

What would someone do if they saw her? Shoot her. Shoot her. Kill her. Kill her. I could hear a crowd chanting their fear into my heart, urging some one with a rifle to kill her, in the rain. I started crying, sobbing.

"Stop it," Little Wolf said, his voice tight. "You can't help her by crying. Look!"

I looked down. In the mud near the rail and crossties, water was seeping into two huge tracks.

Little Wolf squatted and outlined one hand-like print, the four smaller toes, close together, and the larger toe, apart by itself, like a thick thumb. "She stood here. Watching. Over there." He pointed to two more prints, gouges in the mud.

In my mind, I could see Black Diamond, pausing, hesitating, standing for a moment beside the tracks, looking ahead toward the town, a spatter of white houses and brick buildings among oak and sycamore and maple trees, now yellow and red in the evening light.

Little Wolf was trotting ahead, stooping, his head down, his boots squishing in the mud. "She ran this way," he said, pointing at a muddy trail leading toward the town.

The footprints ended at the base of a small hill, plastered with sumac bushes, their leaves red, their berries yellowish orange with black centers. A path of mashed shrubbery clashed up the hill.

"She climbed up here," Little Wolf said. "Didn't even use the steps." His narrow fingers stabbed toward wooden steps.

As we stepped off the last wooden step at the top, my heart jumped in fear. Before us, two-story houses, brick and wood, with screened-in porches and wide lawns, fronted the street. The rain clouds had ripped away from the horizon like torn pieces of crepe paper, showing a purple-black sky beneath the gray, apricot-colored horizon. Fog was circling, drifting among the trees and bushes, like hunters grouping.

"Here." From across the street Little Wolf motioned to me with his hand, and I was following him through front and back yards, running between oak trees and around lilac bushes, dodging flower beds of golden marigolds and red hollyhocks, bordered with small, white wire fences.

Little Wolf stopped at the foot of a brick wall, laced with green and dark purple ivy. Above us twin towers on a house like the decking of a riverboat floated out of the mist. Rainwater gurgled out of the mouths of downspouts. Someone was talking on the other side of the wall.

"Which way?" I asked.

Little Wolf jerked his thumb upward. Then he grabbed some ivy and pulled himself up, rolled his body to the top of the wall and over. I followed, scraping my knee on a broken brick, and jumped, jarring my legs as I thudded into the wet ground.

A thin woman in a dark, purple dress stood in the middle of a back yard, staring at us, her mouth opening and closing rhythmically. Her nose was a slash between two heavy rouge spots, and her chin the tip of a triangle above a high collar. She brandished a rake, its tines mud-crusted, in one hand.

"You there climbing my wall," she said. "Looking for your buddy?" She shook her rake. "A poor idea of a joke—trying to scare me in that silly monkey outfit. Well, your turnip thief's in there. Trapped." She waved her rake toward a small greenhouse in the back of the yard, against an ivy-covered wall.

Little Wolf muttered something, and I stared back at him, thoughts galloping through my head like undisciplined liberty horses racing around the ring.

The woman had frightened her into a greenhouse? What would we do? How could we take her back to the train?

"Well, you two can stand there and think all you want to," the woman said. Red flamed her neck above the high, black collar. "But I've already phoned the sheriff and he's sending over a deputy and then we'll dig up turnips all right. Legal turnips. I'll teach you circus trash to climb my wall and dig up my garden."

A deputy will bring a gun, I thought. Samantha, think. And do something. Quickly.

"Go get her wagon," I said and started toward the greenhouse, my arms and legs shaking with fear and excitement.

Inside the Greenhouse

I walked toward the greenhouse surrounded by dark bushes, its glass panes ghostly, rising out of the black earth and mist against the ivy-covered wall. I knew what I must try, so I crossed my fingers tightly, nervous but hopeful.

I paused in front of a small wood-framed door, its rusted hinges broken back. Some black hairs were stuck in the door jamb. "Black Diamond, it's me." I tried to make my voice sound normal, but it was quivering. "Let's go back to the train. Before the deputy comes."

Plop. Plop. Plop. Water dripped off the glass panes into a red, broken pot, with a rhythmic beat.

"Wraagh?" I called.

She moved inside the greenhouse, a slight rustle. "Wraagh," she called softly to me. She sounded afraid. Was she as frightened as I was?

"It's Samantha. Okay?" Her voice sounded tired, but not angry, I thought. Yet how did a gorilla think, behave?

I didn't hesitate, didn't think about what I was doing, about how much danger I was facing, but dropped to my knees and crawled through the door, keeping my head down.

Inside, I was crawling in a garden, a miniature garden of flowers and plants. Pots filled with ferns and marigolds lined a narrow, gravel pathway. Pots of red geraniums had been brushed aside, knocked over, broken, the matted roots of the flowers tiny white nets in the black soil. The air was moist and warm and smelled of plants and leaves, a thick, heavy smell of earth and decay. It also smelled of Black Diamond's rich, overpowering animal odor.

I kept my face down. "Wraagh?" I called.

"Wraagh." She sounded curious and close. I lifted my head slightly, but I couldn't see her, just a redwood box of yellow pansies with purple faces.

"Wraagh."

Did she sound angry, annoyed? I knew I needed to hurry. I sat up slowly, careful not to move quickly, lifting my face slowly, the blood pounding in my head like a distant drum beat.

Black Diamond sat four feet away in the middle of ferns and white lilies like spurts of white flame. I was looking into her brown eyes. She squinted her eyes slightly and wrinkled her thick brow. I dropped my eyes a little, feeling my face flush. "Easy girl," I said. "I need to help you." I kept my voice soft, trying to make the words soothing, hoping she'd sense me, understand, let me help her somehow before the deputy came with his guns.

"Wraagh?" she replied. Her teeth bit into something, her mouth making a wet sound. Then a hard object bumped against my arm, and I glanced down. The bottom half of a large, purple and white turnip, its top half snapped off, lay beside my leg.

I lifted my head slowly again. Black Diamond was chewing, working her strong jaws, mashing turnip, her head tilted a little, looking in my eyes. Her eyes flashed toward the turnip, and then back to my face.

"A turnip thief. Stealing from gardens, huh?" I asked without moving my eyes. "But you still want to share?" The tension and fear vanished from my shoulders, washing away with the patter of drizzle on the glass.

My fingers touched my damp jeans, the ground, and then the cold turnip, wet where Black Diamond had chomped its top away. I brought the turnip to my mouth and tasted it, looking into her face. Her eyes narrowed. She watched me chew, then dropped her head against her chest, and moved her hands, like an old woman searching for something in her lap.

"Here," I rolled the turnip toward her, between two broken pots. The turnip bumped into one of her mud-covered feet. She picked it up, sniffed it, wrinkling her large nostrils, tossed it in her dark mouth and crunched it between massive yellow teeth.

Outside the greenhouse, a dog yapped in three sharp barks and a siren shrieked, a distant insect's sound. Black Diamond shifted her heavy torso and shoulders and snapped off another bite of the turnip. Hurry, Little Wolf, I thought.

"You've got to come with me," I said. "And not get mad."

Outside, it was nearly dark, the light slipping away like silver water seeping into the ground. Somehow, I needed to force her outside, soon.

I shivered, damp and cold, my legs quivering. Force? I wasn't thinking clearly enough. No one could force her. If I frightened her, she could easily charge through one of the walls, shattering glass, cutting herself. Then the deputy would shoot her and . . .

"Hold on, Samantha. Slow down. Hold on and think," I whispered to myself. I tried to think like Black Diamond, but I couldn't. I felt caged in. Trapped. The way she must feel. The way she had felt her whole life.

I heard voices, one angry, one shrill, arguing. My teeth chattered. I wanted to scream in anger and fear.

"Naw, I'll just go in there and shoot it. That'll solve the problem, real quick."

"Shoot a man, deputy? For stealing turnips?"

"Mrs. Halls, that ain't no carny in there." The voice sounded assured and business like, official, excited. "This here fella's from the circus."

Wood and leather creaked, and horses' hooves plodded over bricks, sharp clacks.

"Where you going with that wagon, bud?" the deputy asked. The voice sounded puzzled.

Little Wolf said, "I'll pull up in front of the greenhouse."

"And ruin my lawn?" Mrs. Hall's voice was shocked. "Just to take a thief away? You don't need a wagon. Walk over there and arrest him, deputy."

"Giddup there, Red. Samantha, here I come," Little Wolf shouted.

I swiveled my head slowly back to face Black Diamond. The black hair along her arms and shoulders, tipped with brown and gray, fluffed out, like the hair on the back of an angry dog. Her heavy eyebrows hooded her brown eyes. She stopped chewing, the tip of a turnip leaf hanging from a corner of her mouth, her face turned toward the sound of voices, listening now to the wagon wheels squishing across the wet lawn.

I knew I had to take a chance, but I was afraid, my heart pounding, my left leg shaking with excitement. I inched forward, sliding through the thick, wet smell of ferns and flowers toward her, keeping my head tucked down, thinking "Please don't run. Don't run. Don't hurt me. Yourself."

"Wraagh." Her voice was softer, a question to me.

Our legs touched. Her leg was shaking too, a shiver that melted into my fear, like a surge of electricity, uniting us as one for an instant. She was afraid and so was I. We were together in our loneliness and fear and friendship.

I felt soft fingers reaching out, touching my leg, and then her fingers brushed my hair, gently, as if the wind had caressed it. I almost cried out, but I didn't. I kept my head down, letting her run her fingertips over my hair, my face. And she dropped her hand on top of my hand, lightly.

Behind me, wood creaked, and a horse snorted. I held my breath and eased my hand into Black Diamond's, feeling the softness of her palm and her hair. Finally, I lifted my face and looked up into her brown eyes, my heart thumping, drowning out the sound of my breathing.

"Wraagh," I cried, shifting to my knees. I pulled slowly, gently with my hand. "Let's go home."

She followed me, letting me lead her through the ferns and flowers and broken pots and through the door of the greenhouse. Outside, the fog had rolled over the garden, swallowing it in whiteness. The old house with its towers and weathervanes and spires hovered above the fog and mist, a steamboat moored in currents of gray and white. It was cold, a damp wetness that made me shiver.

Little Wolf had backed the wagon against the greenhouse and dropped the wagon's ladder. The cage door was open. In the past week, Black Diamond had watched me climb it a hundred times as I had lugged food and water to her cage. Would she climb it now?

We were crouched at the bottom of the stairs. I knew we had to move quickly, before the deputy acted or a noise frightened her.

"Come," I said firmly, tugged at her hand, and stepped on the bottom step, waiting, my arm extended tightly behind me. She didn't move.

I turned. "Dinner?" My voice was shaking, but I tried to question her the way I always said it when I fed her each night.

Still she didn't move. A harsh voice clipped through the fog. She stared at me, looked up at the cage, her eyes wide now, the hair on her back bristling up. She started to tremble. My arm ached.

"Please help me," I said. "Don't run. Hurry up."

Suddenly, she shuffled toward me, balancing with one hand, and we climbed the wagon stairs, quickly, and stepped into her cage. She dropped my hand and scrambled over the floor toward her house, a large, red box, its outside decorated like a castle with battlements and drawbridge. She crawled inside.

As I closed and locked her cage door, I saw her peek out at me from the box, clutching her favorite toy, a stuffed bear, before she hid. My shirt was drenched with sweat, and my legs were quivering. I felt as if I had sprinted a hundred yards while holding my breath. I plopped down on the top of the steps, holding my head between my hands, calming myself down. I stared at my wet, muddy shoes. They reminded me of huge black clown shoes. I laughed until the tears came.

"What's so funny? I had you all covered the whole time." The deputy's face stuck up at me from the fog, a carp gulping air in a dirty river. The deputy's face was double-chinned beneath a round felt hat brim. Water droplets glistened off the star on his heavy chest. He waved a thick-stocked rifle, its bore a black hole, an evil eye. "That monkey weren't goin' anywhere."

"Why did you lock him in the cage?" The woman popped up out of the fog, her white face questioning.

"Mrs. Hall, I told you that's a *real* gorilla—a circus gorilla." The deputy sounded exasperated. He spit a brown stream of tobacco juice against the side of the wagon and stared at me. "He belongs there. With the other freaks. Now, that's a fact."

Little Wolf removed the ladder, stowed it behind the wagon seat, and sat down. "Samantha, climb over here, with me." He patted the leather seat beside him. "We'll leave the turnips here. To talk about it." He clucked to the horses, and the wagon pulled away.

As the wagon wheels slopped through puddles of water, I looked over my shoulder. The deputy and Mrs. Hall were two dark scarecrows, with a rake and a rifle.

The Mechanical Colossus

The next day I was still thinking about how Little Wolf and I had saved Black Diamond. We were in Cherryvale, Missouri. The October sky was blue water, clear and bright, with wisps of clouds swirling like goose down across it. Black Diamond was asleep, one heavy arm hanging outside her box. I leaned against the side of her cage, watching the circus hands unroll the Big Top's wet canvas across a damp baseball field. Under the wagon, Jacko's face was hidden beneath his ragged straw hat: he was flat on his back, snoring quietly. Beside me, Little Wolf was carving the head of a wolf, shaving curls of sweet-smelling pine with his sharp knife.

"Ahem. I hear you brought the snarling beast back into captivity last night—from a turnip patch." I looked down and Colonel Bob stood below me, rolling one end of his waxed mustache between thumb and forefinger, carefully, as if he were fingering the crispness out of a new dollar bill. A small man stood beside him. From beneath the wagon, the snoring caught and stopped. Black Diamond's arm disappeared inside her box.

"Yes, sir."

"Good job. Good job. Oh," he said. "Meet Hirum Peabody. Harum Scarum, we call him. Creator of Mechanical Colossuses and Wonders."

I stared at Hirum Peabody. He was a small man, with skinny legs, drilled into shiny patent leather shoes, with tiny hands that constantly moved, fluttering around his small striped vest and small bow tie like white birds trying to roost. Hard, narrow eyes glittered back at me from beneath the moons of thick spectacles. His hands winged away to his head, and he doffed a small bowler hat and bowed stiffly at the waist.

"Howdy." His eyes roved behind me, over the wagon, toward the cage.

The Colonel rocked back on his heels and nodded toward the wagon. "There it is. What do you think?"

"Ahem," said Hirum, clearing his throat. He stepped backwards, framed his hands and stared at the wagon. Then, he nodded his head. "You've built the frame at least. And what is it you want again, Colonel?"

"Colonel Bob's Mechanical Colossus and Living Tableau to show American Progress—with a capital *P*. The March of Man Through History." The wrinkles on the Colonel's forehead slanted upward as he smiled.

One of Hirum's hands fluttered upward as he removed his bowler and rubbed a bald scalp, between two fringes of thin hair, then patted loose strands into place. "I see, I see. Yes . . . ahem. A little gilt here and there. Ahem. The figures marching across the top. The piston there. It can be done, can be done." He popped his hat back on his head.

"I knew it," the Colonel said, smiling his tight smile. "How long will you take?"

"It's difficult, difficult." Hirum shrugged his skinny shoulders. "I'll need material, help. Help. Eight, maybe ten, weeks at least."

"Ten weeks?" Colonel Bob's face looked like his teeth had cracked a rock from a Cracker Jack box. He sputtered. "But I wanted to close the show in St. Louis in November. That's four, five weeks away."

"Sorry, sorry. Can't be helped, helped. My equipment is here, and you travel all the time. I can't be expected to—"

Colonel Bob looked around at the men carrying hammers and pulling canvas and unloading wagons from the train with mules and horses, barking out their orders. He rubbed his pointed jaw, stroking his white beard to a point. "And if we stay here?"

"Here? Here?" Hirum asked, pointing his finger at the ground like he'd found a strange bug.

"Well, I admit it'd be unusual, resting like this for a while, but," Colonel Bob said slowly, watching the tent crew tightening ropes, "we aren't exactly burning the place up with attendance. The sucker . . . I mean the audience needs a spectacle. Besides I'm planning on next year's tour. Progress. I believe in planning ahead."

"I see, I see. Yes, you need something unusual." Hirum pointed a bony finger at the cage. "Something artistic, *mechanically* unusual to go with that monkey. But soon. Ahem. Ahem." He flapped and lifted his hat over one hand, like a magician hiding and showing a canary.

"That's the ticket all right," Colonel Bob replied.

"If you bring the wagon to my shop in town, I can do it in two weeks. Two weeks. No more."

"Sammy, you and Little Wolf pack your stuff," Colonel Bob ordered.

It's Samantha, I thought. What does it take for him to remember my name? Is this really progress? A Mechanical Colossus and Living Tableau? And now Hirum Peabody. Harum Scarum, Harum Scarum was the boss, the boss.

But Harum Scarum's shop *was* interesting, in a mechanical sort of way. His building, an old, three-story, brick warehouse with crumbling mortar and wire-mesh-covered windows, covered nearly a block of space off Cherryvale's Main Street, the usual small-town string of clapboard store fronts beaded together on a wooden sidewalk.

Once Harum's machine shop had been a brewery, filled with kegs, hanging chains, and copper tubes and vats. But now, the vats, tarnished green and smelling of beer, lounged in a dark corner, retired old, fat grandfathers. Chains dangled from the ceiling, and Harum's engines and tools and workbenches and wheels and junk oiled big spots on the concrete floor beneath two skylights.

Harum used a wooden block and tackle, an iron hook the size of Jacko's number fifteen shoe, and linked small pulleys on a thick, oily chain to hoist Black Diamond's cage off the top of the wagon, to swing it above anvils and forges, and to lower it gently in a patch of sunlight next to a dusty window.

"Didn't even wake up, now did she?" Harum asked Little Wolf and me, rubbing his white hands on a blue oil-and grease-stained pair of overalls, rolled up at the bottoms in small cuffs. "The science of mechanics, mechanics. Now grab that wrench and oil can," he said to me, "and let's give Colonel Bob one of Harum's Mechanical Wonders in less than two weeks."

I didn't do much of the heavy work, and most of the time I didn't know what Harum's mind was scaring up, but I was proud of what we built, at least the cleverness of it. Little Wolf moved around boxes and lumber and wheels, silent and pigeon-toed, watching in the shadows and listening to the chatter of sparrows on the roof, always watching and never trapped between equipment and walls. When Harum asked him, he fetched tools, going to the lumberyard for wood and the hardware store for bolts and nails and odds and ends, but I think he was impressed in his way by the mechanical wonder, too.

While Black Diamond snoozed and eyed us from her cage, we built Colonel Bob's America: the Mechanical Colossus and Living Tableau: The March of Man Through History. Jacko referred to it as The De-evolutionary Colossus of Progress and said what America needed were fewer slogans and more doings. Little Wolf said it took small men to build big ideas. When Colonel Bob wasn't around, we shortened the tableau's name to the Colossus.

At the end of two weeks, Colonel Bob rode Old Charley up to view it. We stood back to admire it, wiping our dirty hands with kerosene rags and staring at our newest audience spectacle. Maybe I had been wrong, I thought.

"Tah-dah, tah-dah. What do you think now?" Harum pushed his wire glasses up on the bridge of his nose with an oil-covered hand. He raised narrow eyebrows at Colonel Bob.

I thought: this little oily magician had waved a greasy pipe wrench over the wagon, and presto, Cinderella's pumpkin had become The March of Man Through History. It stood before us, light from the skylights making all the carvings and colors pop out in the dark warehouse.

"Now that's progress. Like upcoming America, sure enough." Colonel Bob crowed, rocking back and forth in his knee-length riding boots. "Look at that Columbus, will you?"

I knew the crowds would love the Colossus. It looked like an enormous carved jewel box, sitting on four wheels, the wheels spiral sunbursts of color—red and orange and blue. In the center of the wagon, a carved Christopher Columbus, waving a thick Arab sword, was stepping out of a big boat, down in Florida maybe, I guess, because of a few scraggly palm trees, and the Indians were all stretched out in the sand with bunches of apples and watermelons as peace offerings.

"The first Wild West ringmaster," Colonel Bob said, stepping forward and tracing Columbus's face with his fingers. "And his servants." As he looked at the scene, he admired himself in the mirrors around the edge of the carving.

I noticed Little Wolf didn't say anything, but he didn't smile either.

"Had to have the oak scrollwork shipped in. Special order, special order," Harum said, pointing his pipe wrench at the edges of the wagon.

There a swirl of gilded corn leaves and wheat sheaves and hay bundles covered the sides of the wagon and lapped up to the Columbus group. Huge American flags hung like red and white wings from both ends of the wagon.

"Amber waves of grain, grain." Harum said proudly. "Look hard and you'll see some coal mines, ships, and railroads, hiding out. In the leaves. But we didn't want to overdo it."

"Exactly," agreed Colonel Bob. "Exactly. I surely do like that."

The top of the wagon looked like the lid of a jewel box, sort of humped up a little, with more vines and leaves heading for the center piece. When he saw the painting, Colonel Bob stared at it for a long time. A man in a pointed beard and mustache and long flowing hair looked out from the middle of an oyster shell, its yellow scalloped ridges like a sunburst behind his white hat. The man held a rifle in one hand, an olive branch in the other, and sported a million-dollar smile, the self-satisfied look of success.

"Remind you of anyone you know? You know?" Harum asked Colonel Bob.

Colonel Bob studied the painting as if he were admiring a museum piece. He whistled softly. "Very nice, partner. Not too wooden though?"

"No, I don't think so," Harum replied dryly.

"And how does that work?" Colonel Bob pointed at metal pipes, wheels, and levers on top of the wagon.

"That's the best part of my Mechanical Colossus," Harum said proudly, hitching his thumbs in narrow suspenders. "The steam engine bottles Money Medicine."

"Money Medicine?" Colonel Bob scratched his head above one ear and looked puzzled.

"The final key to your evolutionary progress." A small smile flicked across Harum's face, as if he were giving complicated directions to a child and enjoying his confusion. "The gorilla cage goes at one end of the wagon—"

"Oh, now I see. Then the march of progress," Colonel Bob said, interrupting excitedly, "to depict Western man as the superior creature, the lord of civilization."

"Exactly. Exactly."

Colonel Bob pitched his voice louder, and a couple of pigeons cooed and fluttered high above on the skylight. He stabbed the air with his finger. "And it all ends in the machine, the Money Machine."

"Of course."

"But what does it make? I mean . . . not real money?" Colonel Bob's voice sounded now hopeful, now doubtful.

Harum's hands flushed away from his vest where they were nesting and dipped into his pants pockets. "Yes. Real money."

Colonel Bob was breathing heavily now, and his eyes widened, showing their whites. "Real Money?" he yelled, his voice rising.

"Harum's Progress Medicine." Harum shoved a chocolate-brown bottle with a white label toward the Colonel.

"Oh," Colonel Bob sighed, like someone had popped him in the stomach. He held up the bottle, tilting it in the light and stared at it, the way a man with poor eyesight will do.

I stepped closer and read over his shoulder the large letters on the label:

Harum's Spoonful of Success

Cures Colds, Corns, and Sore Feet

The Cheapest Progress You Can Buy

The Colonel narrowed his eyes at Harum. I could tell he was already calculating the price of progress. "You didn't mention this," he said flatly, not smiling now, acting tricked.

Harum smiled and blinked his eyes behind the thick moons of his glasses. "You didn't ask."

Colonel Bob's neck reddened. "What's your cut?"

"One-third of all sales."

"One-third?" Now the tops of the Colonel's ears beneath his hat ignited red. "Outrageous . . . why I'll . . ."

90

"You still owe me for most of the wagon. Consider the one-third extra insurance for me. And I want a down payment in advance," Harum said, jerking his thumb at the wagon behind him, "or I'll remodel your wagon. Down to the wheels." He wasn't repeating himself. His words were as clipped as hard twists with his wrench.

"But it's my wagon, blast you!" Colonel Bob stamped a boot heel on the floor and ground his teeth, his face red.

"Yes, it is your wagon—in my building. Your show in St. Louis starts in two weeks, but I've got a good lawyer waiting downtown for you. That'd be a show the newspapers and public would enjoy. Call it advance publicity."

The Colonel could see that Harum had rolled him up tighter than an old rug in a corner. Harum had the wagon in his warehouse, and the Colonel needed the wagon to make the money to pay Harum.

Colonel Bob examined the wagon as if it were a lame horse, thought a while, and said, "Well, what's in the medicine?"

"Sugar, water, and food coloring."

"That's all?"

"Well, er, a little grain alcohol. For the aches and pains of widda women, of course."

"Of course. It'll sell?"

"The sure-fire progress you wanted. You wanted."

The Colonel stuck out his paw. "Done then. A gentleman's agreement."

"Among honorable men then. Agreed," Harum said. "You can move it tomorrow after we stick the monkey cage back on it and you pay your down payment."

A Meeting

That afternoon, Little Wolf had walked back to help load up for the train trip the next day, Black Diamond and I were the only ones in the warehouse, waiting for him to return. After shoving cabbages and turnips through the bars to Black Diamond, I filled her water buckets.

I was very careful. I unlocked the iron and brass padlock with a key the size of my finger and opened the cage door enough to slide and carry the buckets in, talking quietly to her all of the time, sensing her. I was a little nervous, but it didn't seem to bother her too much. She was eating the tops of turnips and watched me carefully. She acted alert, but not alarmed.

After I put the water bucket inside the door, I eased out, pushing the door behind me, and plopped down in front of the cage to rest, read a newspaper, and watch her.

"Wraagh," I said, and Black Diamond chomped a turnip in two, just below the purple top. "The Gorilla Dream to you is a huge vegetable garden. Turnips and cabbage, I'll bet . . ."

Black Diamond's eyes narrowed.

"Sorry. In Africa. Free, I mean. Out of this cage." I rolled another cabbage head against one of her half-filled water buckets. "You didn't ask about mine."

She scooped up a cabbage, peeled off a layer of leaves, and pushed them in her mouth. Her head was cocked to one side, and she was watching me, her eyes following my hand movements, trying to understand me, I think.

"Okay. I'll tell you. I'd like to go back to school some day. And study animals. Maybe become a veterinarian." I wrapped my arms around my legs, the cage key heavy in my pants pocket.

Black Diamond grunted and looked at the water bucket. "Okay, okay," I said. "In a minute."

I spread open the newspaper, a week-old *St. Louis Post-Dispatch* that Jacko and Little Wolf had argued and fought over for two or three days. A large headline read, "FRENCH HALT GERMAN ADVANCE AT THE MARNE." Beneath this headline, a map showed arrows and lines bumping into each other around towns named Chateau-Thierry, Reims, Meaux.

"They're still fighting by a river called the Marne," I said to Black Diamond. I read, "'The French have pushed the Germans back, away from the Marne, the water that flows through the heart of Paris.' Good. The war will be over soon."

"You ought to try this for breakfast." I ruffled an inside page of the paper in front of her. In an advertisement, a boy held a box of W.K. Kellogg Toasted Corn Flakes over a girl in a wicker chair, an angel in a white lace dress and white patent shoes, the picture of sleepy innocence.

I read out loud, "'NOW WATCH HER WAKE UP.'"

"Wraagh."

"She better wake up," I said. "Miss Sunnydale ought to wake up to a gorilla, like I do, every day." I sounded sarcastic and maybe a little envious for a moment, but I knew I'd never fall asleep in a wicker basket, like a canary in a bamboo cage.

At the end of the warehouse, a door opened and closed quietly behind me. Little Wolf probably had come back, I thought. Now, I'd have to snap the lock shut and water her through the small doors.

I waved my hand at the Colossus, sparkling in the dimness of the warehouse, a rich promise of future success for me or another example of the Colonel's bunkum. Did the Colossus stand for America? For freedom? Progress? Taming the wilderness? Law and order? Those new-fangled electric lights and plumbing? And lots of money?

Maybe it was a lie as Jacko had said. More bunkum. I wasn't quite sure.

"You don't like this progress? Money Medicine? So, who cares if it's mostly sugared water? I wonder who'll sell it. Who'll buy it?"

"Wraagh?" Black Diamond's voice was a question. She'd stopped peeling her cabbage. She wrinkled her nose up, held her head up, and sniffed the air.

The cabbage rolled out of her hand, and hair bristled along her shoulders. She tilted her head downward and parted her lips. Footsteps padded on the concrete behind me. The hair on my neck tingled.

"Hey, you there, chump."

I turned around slowly, not even standing up, the newspaper still in my hand.

A heavy-set man with a pockmarked face, thick hairy arms, and bowlegs smacked an axe handle in an open palm. Behind him, another man with bristling red hair squatted on his heels, a blue line of smoke curling upward from a short cigarette. Next to him, a man as thin as an exclamation point stroked the end of a baseball bat, a thick brown one with scars on it.

"Run along to the other freaks down at the track, boy. We got some business here."

My cheeks flushed. "I'm not a boy," I said, hearing my voice echo in the warehouse. Behind me, Black Diamond growled softly, a warning.

"Hah," the pock-faced one said. "Then you should've been. Some kind of freak watching a baboon cage. It's unreligious."

What was he talking about? I wondered. I slowly stood up, my knees popping, my legs cramped from sitting bowlegged. "You've got the wrong place," I said, holding my hand palm out. When would Little Wolf and Jacko come back?

"No, you've got the wrong town with your S-S-Satanism," the red-haired man said in a high, squeaky voice. Red pimples blistered his face. "Evolution and Darwin. Satanic progress. The church—"

"That's enough, Bill." A wave of the axe handle silenced the squeak. Yellow teeth, stained with tobacco juice, erupted from a fleshy face. The lips curled upward, mockingly. "The community heard that you're hiding a big ape down here, saying we done evolved from him."

I couldn't resist it. "Now, I see. So you three geniuses just slithered from beneath your rock to—"

"Satanic!" Pimples screeched.

I opened my mouth to say something more about their ancestors, but, suddenly, Pock-face jumped at me and grabbed my arm, pinching it tightly beneath dirty fingers with chewed nails. His breath smelled of onions and cabbage and fried meat. He pushed me in front of him, across the floor toward the door. I tried to dig my heels in, but my leather soles slid on concrete.

"Black Diamond! Help," I yelled over my shoulder.

Pock-face laughed, a snuffle, like a pig with its snout buried in the slop, an ugly sound, something broken and sick from inside. "Shut up and get out of here. Back to your circus, you freak." He hissed warm spittle across the back of my neck.

I screamed as loudly as I could, a real glass breaker.

"Grrrr!" Black Diamond roared in rage and fear.

Scar-face spun around, swinging me by the arms with him.

Black Diamond was standing on all fours, throwing cabbage leaves and turnips in the air, her mouth open, baring her teeth. She pounded her chest. "Pock-a-pock-a-pock."

"Big hairy deal," Scar-face laughed and pushed me toward the door.

"Here kitty, kitty." Squatting, Pimples screeched and waved his baseball bat in tight circles at Black Diamond. "We'll be back for you too, you big . . . oh, my God."

I looked up in time to see Black Diamond run into the front of the cage, hitting it with her chest, grunting and growling. The cage wobbled forward, grating across the concrete floor, and the door sprang open, clanking against the floor. She rocketed out the open door, her teeth yellow, her face contorted, and bolted toward me.

An axe handle thudded on the floor and rattled. Someone cried out. Out of the corner of my eye, I glimpsed a shadow, like a bat wing, unfold across a wall and vanish. I was paralyzed, watching her run toward me, an angry black dervish, moving fast, her mouth open, snarling.

She covered the space between us quickly, screaming and roaring all of the way. Suddenly, I came unfrozen and dropped to the floor, tucked myself up into a bundle, and wrapped my arms around my head. She brushed over me, and she screamed and roared again, beside me.

"Pock, pock-pocka-a-pock." Pungent animal musk thickened the air, and her body pressed against me, warm and heavy. I opened my eyes and peeked under my arm.

Black Diamond was standing over me, breathing heavily and growling, the heel of her back foot pressed firmly against my knees, one arm planted in front of my face. Although I was shaking and scared, I felt like a child, protected by her mother, secure and safe. Peering around her arm, I was staring at the frozen statues of Pimples, Scar-face, and the Exclamation Point.

All of them had their mouths open. Their clubs were strewn around them. The Exclamation Point held his arms wrapped around his body, shaking uncontrollably, a thin arrow of terror. Pimples was kneeling, his hands folded before his mouth like a small tent, his mouth mumbling. Scar-face held his hands high in the air, like a bank robber does when he faces a gun.

"Easy. Easy." Scar-face said. "Nice monkey, nice b-i-g monkey."

Black Diamond rumbled.

I found my voice. "Back off, or she'll eat you."

The thin man turned and ran, clawed open the door, and slid into the sunlight.

"Unscientific," a cold voice said. A shadow flicked across the floor, vanished.

Black Diamond rocked forward on her arms and growled again, the rumble deep in her chest.

Pimples was praying out loud now, begging for forgiveness for all of his sins—drinking, cursing, and other things— promising all kinds of things I knew he could never deliver.

"Easy, easy. No hard feelings." Scar-face moved stiffly backwards, keeping his shaking hands in front of himself, as if trying to ward off a blow, shouldered his way through the door opening, and then disappeared. I could hear shouts and then his feet in the gravel, running.

Black Diamond snarled.

"You've got to get up," I said to the converted sinner, feeling my legs starting to shake, the way I always do, after I've been frightened.

Somehow Pimples pulled himself slowly up and walked stiff-legged out the door, his hands still upraised, and kicked the door closed. I still huddled under Black Diamond, shaking, but safe.

A Warning

"You what?" Colonel Bob asked, shaking his head in disbelief.

He threw his arms in the air as if he were signaling for a crowd to applaud a clown.

I hung my head, glancing at Jacko and Little Wolf. The inside of Colonel Bob's wagon pressed around me, like a cage, too warm, too confining. I felt like running, slamming the door behind me, and never returning. The frozen eyes of the gorilla head seemed to bore into me. "I left the cage door unlocked," I repeated.

"Why? Stupidity. Girl, what do you think you are? An animal trainer? *That's my gorilla.* My property." His index finger punctuated each word. "*My gorilla! My property!*" Red streaks of anger brushed Colonel Bob's cheek, and he twirled the ends of his mustache into dagger-sharp points.

"Don't be too hard on her," Jacko said. "I'm to blame. Should have been there." His voice was gravelly. He looped his thick arms across his faded blue work shirt, ready to defend me.

"She was strong," Little Wolf said, the wrinkles crinkling his leathery face. He smiled as if he were someplace else, watching a scene from a distance, thinking about it. "Like my daughter once when she faced the mountain lion."

Colonel Bob pulled his white cowboy hat off and rubbed his fingers through his hair, showing pink scalp beneath long, iron-gray strands. He glanced at a reflection of himself in a window, frowned, and then patted his hair down, carefully.

"We're lucky," he said. "Nobody was hurt." He looked puzzled for an instant, his brows knifed together. "I'd have thought that big ape would've plucked them apart like chicken wings." He stared at me. "And you're lucky."

"Yes, sir," I said. I really wanted to say, "Black Diamond is my friend, and she's more than property, and she was protecting me." But I didn't. I still respected him, his ideas, and I wanted to see his circus succeed and grow. Besides, I wouldn't have gained anything by arguing with him then, trying to explain what I thought. Colonel Bob always knew when he was right and everyone else was wrong.

"You said the monkey just guarded you? Stood over you? Why?" Colonel Bob asked, pulling his eyes upward in doubt. He fished a cigar out of a wooden box, its lid carved with circus animals, twirled it under his nose, and nipped off the end of it with his pen knife.

Okay, I thought. I will tell you about Black Diamond, explain everything, about how I've worked with her, about how I thought she talked once in her way, about how I feel about her. I opened my mouth, and Jacko coughed. I glanced at him, and he shook his head, slightly.

"Some of us sense animals more." Little Wolf stared to one side of Colonel Bob.

"Baloney," Colonel Bob said, sniffing his cigar. "I sense progress with a big *P*. Money with a big *M*. The future! And we won't reach that with a gorilla maiming our customers. You want progress, don't you?" His blue eyes stared at me. "With Colonel Bob's Wild West Show?"

I understood the threat in his question. "Yes, sir."

"Then stay out of that gorilla cage and keep the door locked." He twirled his cigar with a flourish, dramatically, and a smile snaked across his face and crawled under his mustache.

"Yes, sir," I repeated myself.

"Another thing. We need that gorilla. For Har . . . Colonel Bob's Mechanical Colossus and Living Tableau. *He's my property.* And if you want to be part of the display you'll follow orders and keep your place. Do you understand?"

"Yes, sir," I replied, feeling my face flush. I wasn't ashamed now, just angry that he didn't want to listen to me, didn't care what really had happened in the warehouse, how Black Diamond had protected me.

The Colonel picked up a red and gray ledger book and waved it at us. "So go help 'em finish loading. We've got a show in Jefferson City in two days. This train leaves in an hour. I've bills to pay."

Outside, I walked with Jacko and Little Wolf toward our wagon and the menagerie. I felt down, alone, and I wanted to quit, to blow the circus. And I was confused about how I felt about Colonel Bob. I wanted to believe in him, to work hard, to make our circus bigger, better than the usual flea-bitten mud show.

"I've about had it with Colonel Bob," I said, as we stopped to check again on Black Diamond and the other animals. Their cages were firmly lashed on top of the railroad car. After the railroad accident we'd doubled the number of hemp ropes. "I'm sick of the way he treats me. The way he feels about Black Diamond."

"Samantha, we've got to go forward," Jacko said. He leaned toward me, his hair wiry cotton beneath his battered cavalry hat. "Forward is not backward. Right?"

Little Wolf didn't say anything.

I looked up at the Colossus, covered with a green tarp, bumpy, like a prehistoric lizard with its yellow wagon tongue lapping out. Through an opening in the canvas, I could see Black Diamond snoozing away, on her back, one foot in the air, a stack of vegetables beside her, ones Little Wolf and Jacko had piled in the cage as a treat. I knew it was their way of saying thanks for helping me.

"I don't think the Colonel needs to be so . . . well, so, cheap about it is all," I said.

Little Wolf and Jacko waited for me as I searched for my words. "He acts as if only his dreams matter. Like we're so much extra baggage on his private circus train."

"Then what's your dream?" Jacko asked me.

"I think my dream is more than money, more than cages, more than . . . more than a circus," I said, surprised at how I blurted out my idea.

Jacko pushed a coal cinder around with a scuffed boot, driving it before him like he was herding a black doodlebug. I could see him commanding a group of buffalo soldiers, trying to decide which path to follow. "I think I know what you're talking about. More than a circus?"

"Something bigger," I replied. I thought a while. "More like a large village where everyone acts friendly and it's not so cold at times."

"How big would you make this village?"

"Just enough to fit all of the misfits of the world in it."

"It'd be a durned big circus," Jacko said. "A regular three-ringer."

"What's a circus to you," Little Wolf asked me.

"Excitement. Make-believe. A place for people to forget," I replied.

Jacko said, "Shore nuff. It's all of that." He flicked the doodlebug with the toe of his boot.

"But I just don't like what the Colonel's trying to make them believe." I pointed at the yellow tongue of the Colossus.

"What's that?" Little Wolf asked.

"The Wild West. All the gunfights with Indians. Always controlling things—the dog acts, putting Black Diamond in a cage." I felt odd saying these things.

"Girl, you're talking about progress." Jacko snorted. "About his future now."

"Maybe. I don't know exactly. It's just the history and science and technology and money all wrapped up together." I made some kind of vague gesture. "The Colossus. Little Wolf. Black Diamond. That sugared one-dollar snake oil."

"The Marne?"

"The Marne?" I didn't understand.

"The trenches. That old Archduke Ferdinand shot up in his fancy touring car. Bang. Like the biggest three-ring circus."

Jacko reached over and picked up the bug and watched it crawl across his palm. "You'd need to stretch a mighty canvas to get all the misfits under one Big Top."

"Misfits? We're a pretty small bunch of misfits," I replied.

Jacko gently placed the bug on a yellow head of Johnson grass. "Who's the misfits?"

Little Wolf held up his hand. "Enough of this." He smiled. "The girl is progressing."

The train lurched a bit, and we scrambled to climb aboard. "You ain't' blowin' this show, are you, Samantha?" asked Jacko, a worried look on his face as we boarded the train.

"No," I said. "I'm responsible for Black Diamond. Besides, misfits should stay together."

Jacko just grinned.

Parade Time

Colonel Bob's Incredible Circus, Menagerie, and Wild West Show—The Greatest Train and Wagon Show in the World had never visited Jefferson City, Missouri, and Jefferson City wasn't family.

I could feel a sullenness, an unhappiness in the air when our train rolled into the railroad backyards in the early morning. It wasn't the narrow, brick streets guarded by heavy sycamores and thick elms or the squat brick houses with broken porches and cracked windows, the paint peeling away like raw sores. It was something else that we sensed, almost smelled—a discontent, a hatefulness, perhaps an evil lurking.

We unloaded the wagons from the train, lined them up for the Grand Parade, and watched the sunrise, a cold redness slipping around gray boulders of clouds. Standing in dew-soaked grass, we ate pancakes floating in maple syrup and drank warm coffee from Cookie's campfire.

"Definitely unfriendly," Jacko said, aiming his fork at a pile of litter tossed against a vacant house, its windows empty, dark holes. "You don't look so friendly yourself, Little Wolf."

Little Wolf wrapped both hands around his tin cup, letting the steam curl around his face, and nodded in agreement, but he wasn't happy, leaning against the Colossus, dressed in full battle gear. He wore a war bonnet of eagle feathers that draped down his back and buckskin clothing, a fringed shirt with animal prints across the front and an orange sun in the middle, split by a black lightning bolt. Red and yellow and black stripes marked his cheekbones. His heavy rifle leaned against a wheel, a black rod.

"How-um, Blackman." Little Wolf imitated a cigar-store Indian with upraised hand, palm out.

Jacko grimaced at the joke. He arched his back, stretched stiffly, walked away, and looked up at the Colossus.

"Think this will cheer the town up, Samantha? Cheer us up?" He waved his cup at the wagon.

The sun was spraying light across the Colossus, and it was beautiful. The painted woodwork of the wagon glimmered, a huge polished fairy chest. The mirror surrounding the scene of Columbus's landing looked like an oval diamond. From a distance, Columbus almost looked heroic, waving his sword, with the Indians piled in front of him. The mirror reflected Little Wolf, Jacko, and myself, a group to one side. Above the mirror Colonel Bob smiled in the painting, clutching his rifle and olive branch, long white hair like flames.

On the top, Black Diamond's cage perched like a cabin on the stern of an old sailing ship. My old friend was sitting in her favorite corner, a dark shape, watching us quietly. An empty pedestal surrounded by a painted handrail stood even with the top of her cage. Then, Harum's metal handiwork anchored the center of the wagon: a tree of brass pipes, tubes, gears, sprockets, whistles, and bells. To the right of the brass and iron stood a pulpit, bright yellow, with a large, green dollar bill painted in the middle.

A white canvas stretched across the wagon, under the cage, the machinery, and the pulpit, above the golden carvings and mirror. It read in capital letters: THE MECHANICAL COLOSSUS AND LIVING TABLEAU: THE MARCH OF MAN THROUGH HISTORY.

"You'd think the Colonel could abbreviate it some, wouldn't you?" Jacko said and laughed.

"Too big an idea," Little Wolf replied.

Later that morning, I waited for the parade to begin, dressed in a black tuxedo with cummerbund and a bow tie, standing behind the pulpit, with a box of Harum's Money Medicine at my feet. Little Wolf climbed up on the pedestal, rifle in hand, and Jacko disappeared through a trap door inside the wagon, carrying his toolbox.

I said to myself, "This should be interesting."

We rolled along behind our black horses in red tassels, impatient, talking, toward the long Main Street, a dirt road with two-story wooden storefronts standing on end like big boxes. A lot of people crowded next to the hitching rails and wagons—farmers in heavy boots, women in calico patterns, and kids jumping up and down, running out in the middle of the street and then back to their parents' feet.

As we started up the street, Jacko fired up Harum's Colossus. Sounding like a fat man puffing and wheezing up a tall flight of stairs, the Colossus roared to life: wheels rolled, levers turned, pistons pumped—and steam billowed out a bright, red, miniature smokestack in the middle. And whistles and pipes and bells shrieked and bonged and hooted.

It was Pandemonium, with a capital *P*.

The loud noise startled me so much that I clapped my hands over my ears and dropped a brown bottle of Money Medicine between my feet, breaking it and soaking one pants leg. People went wild over the Colossus—everyone, men, women, children, animals. Horses whinnied and lunged on the ends of harnesses and bridles, kicking, bucking. A yellow cat meowed, darted down a board sidewalk, and shot into the door of a dry goods store, rotating his tail like a propeller.

Suddenly, inside of her cage, Black Diamond roared, a howl of anger. From my pulpit, I could see the bars of her cage. Her hands grabbed bars, tightened, then moved to another pair, testing them. The whistle shrieked again, and Black Diamond bellowed.

"Hey, look at the gorilla," someone yelled from the crowd. "The rascal's going crazy."

"Wait till the Spring Hill boys hear about this." A man with a strawberry birthmark staining his face laughed and spit a stream of tobacco between his feet.

A boy in a dirty pair of overalls scampered beside the wagon and jumped up and down, dangling his arms and beating his chest, shaking his fist at Black Diamond. An old man doubled over in laughter and slapped his knee, straightened up, slung a jug over his arm, and swigged a drink.

"Hey, it's a circus, boys. Let 'em have it." Plop. A rotten tomato splattered against the pulpit, spraying me with smelly juice. I glanced ahead. The town's main street was just two blocks long, and we'd covered only half of that distance. Hurry up, I thought.

A man with a matted black beard trotted beside the wagon, laughing and screaming a war whoop. "How, Big Chief. You make 'em war. Take 'em scalps." He carried something dark in his hand, held closely to his hip.

The whistle shrieked. Black Diamond screamed and smashed something metal against the bars of her cage.

"Watch out," I yelled to Little Wolf, pointing to the man.

Suddenly, the man stopped running, wound up, heaved a rock. Little Wolf ducked down. The rocked missed him by ten feet and clanged off a brass pipe and clattered across wood and bounced off the wagon.

"Hurry up," I shouted to the driver. "Quicker."

He looked back, his face white, and then snapped the reins to the four horses. They broke into a trot, a canter, a gallop.

I held on to the pulpit, watching the townspeople below me shake their fists at us as we dashed by. The whistles and chimes stopped blowing. The wagon rocked and pitched like the Santa Maria tossing in stormy seas. I looked back at Little Wolf. He had jumped off his pedestal and was crouching by Black Diamond's cage, his rifle in his arms, scanning the roofs of houses and stores as we charged ahead. We didn't pause at the fairgrounds but rattled down a brick side street to the train.

As soon as we stopped beside our flatcar, Little Wolf climbed down. "In America the Wild West never dies." He pulled a brown paper sack from his buckskin shirt and put it to his mouth.

I climbed out of my pulpit and hurried past Harum's machinery to Black Diamond's cage. She was standing in front of her sleeping box, legs planted, arms outstretched. Her mouth was open and her eyes wide. She was breathing heavily, her tongue out. The inside of her cage was a mess: pans were dented and scattered about, cabbage and turnip greens covered the floor, a wooden box lay shattered in the corner.

"Howdy, she's shore mad," Jacko said, coming up to me. He looked exhausted, dirt and oil streaks grooving his face. He struck a heavy finger in one ear, twisted it, and shook his head. "My head feels like someone pounded on it. Sorry. I couldn't stop the noise after I fired her up."

"Some Colossus," I snapped. I was mad. I scraped some rotten lettuce leaves and squashed tomatoes off bars. "If that's progress I . . ."

Jacko pulled an oily engineer's cap off his head and mopped his face with a red bandanna. "I don't think it's exactly what the Colonel had in mind."

"If he even has one."

"Easy, Sammy."

"Samantha, please!"

"Don't say anything. I'll talk to him about putting Black Diamond on the Colossus." Jacko arched his eyebrows, pieces of cotton.

Colonel Bob and Little Wolf, carrying axe handles and baseball bats, walked toward us, their heads together, talking. As Jacko and I climbed off the wagon, I noticed some of our men squatting on their heels in clumps of tall, brown grass, alert.

"Saddle up," Colonel Bob said to our driver, nodding at the railroad flatcar. "We'll be in St. Louie tomorrow night. Where they'll understand us. Educating them to new ideals." He spat. "These country bumpkins wouldn't appreciate a good circus no more. . . no more than that gorilla up there."

"Ideas you meant?" I asked.

Colonel Bob frowned at me. "No. I mean ideals. Something to dream about."

"Looks like they're pretty fixed with the same old ideas," Jacko said. "It's gonna take a lot of educating."

I started to say something, but Jacko stepped on my toe, hard.

Colonel Bob looked at us and clapped his hands. "Er, the show must go on, right?" He smiled weakly and glanced over his shoulder. "Reminds Little Wolf and me of the old days. Posting guards. But I don't expect any more trouble from those jackasses. These country fools have enjoyed their last laugh on us."

I couldn't restrain myself. I coated my sentence with sarcasm. "We're evolving on to bigger and better business—with a capital B, aren't we?"

Colonel Bob spun around, anger branded in his face. "One more word out of you and you stay here." A muscle jerked beneath his eye.

Behind me, Black Diamond moved in her cage. I pinched my leg, didn't say a word, and thought of half-a-dozen replies, all of them about his ideas, ideals, and circus.

"Yes, siree," I said and studied the grass between my shoes, submissive, acting the part he wanted me to play.

"Now, load up," Colonel Bob said to everyone. "I'll work out the details better for everyone in St. Louie." He walked off, rapping his baseball bat against his leg.

"Is Black Diamond an everybody?" I asked.

"Now honey, don't you fret none," Jacko said.

"I doubt it. But I'm sure it'll be progress." I clanked a chain around one of the wheels of the Colossus. "What's progress anyway?"

"That's a good question," Jacko replied.

"Where are we progressing and to what?"

"Does seem like the same old story, now don't it? You don't worry about it and grab the end of that tarp. Let's blow this place and get on to St. Louie."

Caged

"You'll be in the cage. During the spectacle," Colonel Bob said, smirking, his eyes glinting. "The little St. Louie gorilla. You've earned your progress with a little *p*."

Standing in a shadow of his wagon with Jacko and Little Wolf, I was flabbergasted. What was Colonel Bob talking about now, I wondered?

We were in the outskirts of St. Louis, near the railroad yards off Broadway. In front of us, circus hands were hoisting the Big Top, under a cloudless sky of bright sunshine, in some empty lots. Brown apartment buildings with soot-stained bricks and green roofs pressed against the lots next to some rundown warehouses. Clotheslines with dresses and underwear sagged between buildings. The air smelled of fried bacon and fried potatoes and steamed cabbage. A couple of kids, holding baseball bats and worn mitts, watched the men struggling with the tent.

"You're changing the Colossus, then?" Jacko asked.

"Tonight?"

Colonel Bob turned to him. "I'm taking your advice. The gorilla's too dangerous riding around on Harum's wonder. The noise will drive him crazy. Once was enough."

"What about me? Where's my place?" Little Wolf asked. The neck of a bottle peeked out of his back pocket.

"No, you stay on the pedestal. We need to play up the Wild West idea. Show these city folk something more than cigar-store Indians in their tobacco stores." Colonel Bob looked smug, satisfied.

Little Wolf started to say something, but the Colonel cut him off with a wave of his hand. "I know. I know. Of course, it is not right, but people pay to see it." He rubbed his thumb and forefinger together in little circles.

Jacko said, "I could use an extra hand below in the Colossus."

Colonel Bob ignored the comment.

"We'll park the wagon before the show begins and sell Money Medicine."

"And Black Diamond?" I asked.

"You'll exhibit him in the menagerie tent before the main show. In the grand entry, we'll pull her around on another wagon. Away from the Colossus," he said, "Then, we'll park him off to one side at the other end. People can watch him and the clowns between acts. Keep them busy."

Jacko started to say something, but, quickly waving his hand, the Colonel stopped him from speaking. "You just run the Colossus."

"In the tent? Doesn't that violate city codes . . . I mean, it's dangerous."

The Colonel smiled and rolled his cigar between his lips and stroked his beard into a point. "I've taken care of it." He moved his thumb and forefinger together, rubbing imaginary money.

"But . . ."

"That's enough, Jacko. Big circuses run their steam engines all the time. You know what I like about showing in a big city? A big city is a lot of little towns packed together. We don't have to travel so far to set up, so we save traveling expenses. We should make a killing here."

Later, Jacko, Little Wolf, and I walked over to the menagerie tent to check on the animals.

"So, Samantha, you're finally going to make the center ring," Jacko said. His gold tooth flashed, but he sounded distracted, as if he were thinking about a problem.

"As a gorilla." I laughed, but in an odd way I felt flattered even though the Colonel was going to put me in a cage. Even after all of my disappointments, I clung to my dream of starring in the center ring.

"You're going to do it?" Little Wolf sounded surprised.

I didn't answer too quickly, but dodged Gary the Balloon Man, holding a dozen red and yellow balloons in one hand and carrying an armload of stuffed alligators and elephants in the other.

If I quit, what would happen to Black Diamond? Running away wouldn't free me from my obligations to her and my friends. If I stayed, I could watch over her in the menagerie tent, and sitting in the wagon under the Big Top during the show probably wouldn't bother her much. She'd retreat inside her box and sleep and ignore the crowds. Wearing a gorilla outfit wasn't riding the stagecoach, but I had played a joey, so I could growl and thump my chest, make believe for a while.

"I don't have any choice."

"We all must choose sometime," Little Wolf said. His voice sounded slightly slurred. "Except maybe Black Diamond. She didn't have a choice. She can't choose now." His eyes glinted when he looked at me, challenging me to do something.

I felt confused. What did he want me to do? Steal Black Diamond and run away?

"Well, she's not my gorilla. He owns her," I said defensively, uncertain what Little Wolf wanted of me.

"That's the problem with America," Little Wolf said, shaking his head. "Everyone *owns* someone because everyone *owes* someone."

We were standing in front of one of the sideshows, the Colonel's Palace of Mirrors. For a Liberty head nickel, a person could walk around inside and see his reflection warped by different-shaped mirrors. Little Wolf was staring at a dwarf—himself—a short Little Wolf under a sign that read "See the Real You!!!" He spat on the ground and walked away, leaving Jacko and me together.

"I don't like it," Jacko said.

"Don't like what?" I asked.

"Taking the Colossus under the Big Top."

"Why not?"

Jacko poked his hands in the back of his overalls and shrugged. "There's a boiler cooking the steam for the Colossus, and we're in a tent."

"So?" I still didn't understand what he meant.

"There aren't many exits and . . ."

"You're afraid of a fire?" My voice must have sounded disbelieving.

"That boiler gets pretty hot in the Colossus." Jacko's face looked worried. "All of those people. Probably I'm too nervous. That last parade, I guess."

"It'll get better," I said, touching his arm. "At least you won't have to sit inside the Colossus and listen to the bells."

"You're right about that," he said and laughed. "Now I can go nuts on the outside with everyone else. But still . . . aw, let's check the animals."

A Fist Fight

That same day Jacko and I thought we'd feed the animals, rest, and play a game of gin rummy off our orange-crate table, but Colonel Bob opened the gates to the midway, the carnival rides, and the menagerie. He wanted to excite the kids who had been peeking through the fence all day so they'd spread the word about next afternoon's show under the Big Top.

Just before Colonel Bob closed the gate three boys and a girl, loud and obnoxious, crowded into the menagerie tent, wearing leather jackets and the same type of heavy wool caps. A thin man with a knee-length fur coat, gold-headed cane, and black gloves slipped in after them, but he stood off to one side, examining the exhibits. Jacko and I stopped shuffling cards and posted ourselves behind the rope we'd stretched in front of the cages.

"Hey, Mick, look at the rubes—the an-u-mals too," a tough-looking boy with long black hair curling over his collar said.

"Hee-haw. Hee-haw," Mick said. He flipped his arm off his girlfriend, a thin blonde. Her lipstick bled off her mouth into heavy makeup.

The tough saw Black Diamond in her cage in the corner. "Hey, lookee at the gorillee." He laughed at his joke, a line of decaying teeth showing. "You, hayseed." His beady eyes were challenging me. "You feed this monster?"

"Yes," I said, staring at the ground, not wanting to talk, trying to avoid his eyes. I could smell fish, fried potatoes, and bad breath.

"Growl for us," Mick said. He dropped his hands, jumped up and down, and then scratched his sides with both hands. His girlfriend laughed.

"No," I said, feeling my arms tighten.

Mick turned to another friend, a lanky boy, younger, probably sixteen or seventeen, in a dirty green shirt, brown dungarees, and a pair of knee-length boots. He kept his hands in his pockets. "How about you, nigger?"

Jacko didn't say a word but stared straight ahead, his arms rigid at his side, as if he were standing at attention, on a parade ground.

"An-u-muls-s can't talk, can's they?"

"They struggle with it," I said, as sarcastically as I could, but I don't think he understood.

"Betcha I can make 'em," Mick said, jerking on the rope and stooping under it, before Black Diamond's cage. When he stood up from beneath the rope, he held something in a doubled-up fist.

I was so mad I didn't wait for him to lift his hands. I hit him on the point of the chin, throwing my weight into the punch. He dropped straight backwards, over the rope, like a gunny sack of potatoes, and didn't move.

The other bullies looked at Mick asleep on the floor for a second, and then the fight began. They swarmed at me. I unloaded a couple of pretty good licks before two of them tackled me. I heard Black Diamond roaring and Jacko shouting. The bullies smelled of unwashed bodies, heavy, sweet aftershave, and stale beer—and then I felt a buzzing in my head, a light floating, and I sailed away into darkness.

Next, Jacko was patting my face with a cool, wet towel, and Black Diamond was growling someplace far away through the dizziness. Jacko's face snapped into view, silhouetted against tent canvas.

"Child, why'd you do that?" he asked, his strong arms cradling me, holding the towel against my face. I touched my cheek. It hurt and felt the size of an English walnut. He helped me sit up.

"How'd I do?" I asked, trying to stand.

Jacko's strong arms held me down. "Just a minute. Fine, fine. The 10th Cavalry could've used you. But it ain't right. A girl fightin' like that."

"He asked for it," I said. "And why not? Boys and men fight all the time."

"Shore enough. And that's the problem. Don't I know it."

"There *is* a problem." I couldn't see him, but I knew Colonel Bob's voice. His voice sounded excited, high and fast, the way it does when he's working on an idea out loud.

Oh great, I thought. I had uncorked more than a punch this time. Now, I'm fired, in the middle of St. Louis, without money or a place to go.

"Quite a left hook. A dandy. Good swing for a girl." Colonel Bob squatted in front of me, holding his white hat in one hand. The pink of his scalp was glistening through his plastered-down hair. He smelled of stale cigars and musky aftershave.

"I'm sorry. I lost my temper . . ."

Colonel Bob waved his hand for silence, as if he were quieting a crowd for the next performance. "No, no. I saw it all. Just came in before you Arkansawed him. You reminded me of me, when I was a young sprout. But that gorilla." He bobbed his head toward Black Diamond's cage, like he was sniffing something in the air.

My shoulders ached, but I swiveled my neck and head a bit. Black Diamond was squatting in the middle of the cage, glaring. Her mouth hung open, and her eyes glimmered in the fading light, yellow, like a cat's eyes. Colonel Bob shifted his weight, and she moved slightly forward, her eyes narrowing.

"Wouldn't he like to meet me now? Does he act like that when someone bothers you?" the Colonel asked.

"She. Like what?" I asked, not seeing then what he was thinking.

"Mad. Ready to kill."

"I wouldn't use that word," I replied. "Protective describes her better."

"The same as the warehouse?"

"Yeah, I guess so."

Then his face lit up in a funny sort of smile, as if he saw someone who owed him a favor, and he remembered something unpleasant about him. Then the smile slid off his face like a sidewinder. "Maybe I'd better think more about this again. Can you make him mad anytime?"

I felt a sickness in my stomach, the same one you feel when you hear bad news, news of a friend's sickness. My head was throbbing and my face ached, but I could sense another piece of the Colonel's progress coming. "It's not good to rile her up," I said.

The Colonel's face went flat, expressionless. "But can you?"

"Don't hurt her," Jacko said.

"Not hurt her. Sort of excite her."

I didn't even hesitate. "I won't. It's not right and it's not fair."

"Samantha, I decide what's fair in this circus," he said and stood up, his knee joints cracking. I think that was the first time he ever recognized me as a woman, called me by my true name, until later when he really needed me, and then I couldn't help him.

He studied Black Diamond for a minute. "This menagerie's not carrying its weight," he said to Jacko. "No wonder people won't pay to come in. Attendance is down. That gorilla's sleeping too much in his cave, or whatever that shelter is. People want to see a killer, not a sleeper. Stir him up some."

"How?" Jacko asked, a muscle in his jaw twitching. He glanced at me.

"With a stick—or something. I don't care how you do it, but I need a mad gorilla to excite people, to get them to pay." Colonel Bob walked stiffly toward the entrance of the tent. In the fading light, his face hovered above the whiteness of his buckskins, like a phantom in smoke or a dim memory from the past. "When I tell you to do something, do it." he pointed his arm at Jacko and then at me. He dropped it and stalked out, in a bow-legged strut.

Jacko led me to the orange crate, swept off the cards, and helped me to sit down. "And what if I won't?" I asked Jacko.

"Child, most of the time in this life, we need to take orders." Before me, he was a black idol, a father I needed, not just an old buffalo soldier, now a discarded circus worker.

"Well, I'm not."

"Sometimes?"

"Never."

He was silent for a while, breathing heavily beside me. "Some advice then?"

"Okay."

"Think of this gorilla. What's old Black Diamond gonna do without you if you blow this circus?"

"I'll steal her." Of course, I knew I couldn't steal her. I was so upset I spouted off the first idea that weaseled into my mind.

Jacko snorted, like a horse does when it sucks dust up its nostrils. "What would you feed her? How would you carry her cage? On your back?"

"I'll buy her, then."

"With what?"

I rubbed the back of my neck. "Okay, okay. I'll think of something. Later. But I refuse to make her mad," I said. "And I don't care what the Colonel said."

Jacko patted my shoulder, softly. "We'll think of something. Both of us, tomorrow. Let the Colonel sleep. Sometimes, he works himself up too much. Always does. Progress, you know."

I knew he was winking at me, our we'll-out-fox'em-together-secret, but I couldn't lift my neck and I didn't feel like joking with him. I knew the Colonel wouldn't change his mind. He really intended to shock Black Diamond, to turn her into a sideshow freak for a few more measly bucks. But I also knew I wouldn't shake the stick for the Colonel, wouldn't poke Black Diamond. I also realized I needed to think of some plan, to do something, and to do it in a hurry.

Center Ring

Early the next morning, I woke up, groggy, with a splitting headache, my blue and white quilt knotted around my legs. I unwound my sheet, rolled out of my bunk bed, and opened the door to my cubicle a crack, looking for Little Wolf and Jacko in the narrow room of our wagon.

Their beds were empty, Little Wolf's neatly made as always, Jacko's with his red covers stripped off, a bar of bright sunlight lying across his mattress like a wedge of copper. He's blown the circus, I thought. Left me. For a second my pulse raced, but then I remembered that he'd helped me to bed and returned to sleep on a cot next to the animals. And then I remembered my fight with Mick and my argument with Colonel Bob.

Before I walked over to the cook tent for breakfast, I looked in a cracked mirror, a small, cheap one, wedged in a corner above our washbasin. I talked with myself, between me and the image of myself.

"You're changing," I said. Physically, I had changed that summer. The sun and wind had browned me, making my blue eyes seem darker, the green specks in them like shards of carnival glass. The weather had bleached my blonde hair, whitening my bangs.

My face had narrowed, become even more angular in places, more adult, more assertive, not so childish.

If, as the poets say, the eyes are windows revealing the soul, then I was peeking at a different Samantha Starr.

"What's the big difference?" I asked myself, trying to speak about the change I saw in the mirror.

"I'm more independent," I said, brushing my bangs away from my forehead. "Not so innocent. Not so hopeful."

I straightened up the collar of my wrinkled blue work shirt. "And not so trustworthy, so naive. More assertive." I thought of the summer and of everything that had happened, of Colonel Bob's ideas for progress and the American Dream and Black Diamond.

Now I felt older, in the same way as when a child I'd discovered that Bonzo the clown wasn't only a carefree clown but an older man, wearing a polka-dotted costume with big orange shoes, only playing at make-believe, trying to make people in the audience forget their cares—and running from his own drinking. Then I realized that paint and cold cream were a mask, makeup that hid him and confused me, unless I looked at him more closely. When I did, I found something more than whiskey hidden in brown paper sacks, something more important than his act—a person who needed a friend.

"What did you find this time?" I asked my reflection, leaning close to the mirror to look into the green flecks of my eyes.

"What I value the most. Jacko. Little Wolf. Black Diamond. Things that are important to me. Friends. Respect and love. My village."

Yet I couldn't see all of the new Samantha, or look into a crystal ball to see the future. I still felt confused about a lot of things. What should I do next? Stay with the circus or leave? Had I been serious when I said I'd steal Black Diamond? What would I do if Colonel Bob ordered me to shock Black Diamond?

I probably could never answer all my questions. I probably would never straighten me out, I thought, but at least I felt I owned a center—like a center tent peg running down the center of me—to anchor my beliefs to. Although I didn't know how to hitch all the ropes together yet, to tie off all the loose strands of unforeseen events, I felt the pole rooted in my soul and core and heart, holding me in place.

I picked up two other strands that afternoon—big ones, thick with humiliation and money.

A work gang had moved Black Diamond's cage early that morning to a smaller wagon, parked in front of the Colossus. The weather was hot. I was sitting in the shade of the Colossus, by a sunburst wheel, waiting to get behind my money box, looking at Black Diamond crouched in the corner of her old, small cage, squeezed into a sliver of shade, swatting every once in a while at buzzing flies. She looked miserable and unhappy.

"Here, this is for you," Jacko held a large, brown bag. He tossed a black, fuzzy costume at my feet. "It shorely beats a stick."

I stood up and held the outfit against my chest, matching the arms against my arms, its legs against my legs. Two rubber hands with thick fingers like breakfast sausages dangled beyond my hands.

Jacko grinned and pushed his cigar down his lips to the corner of his mouth. "Colonel Bob was just spouting the other night. Needed time to think about it. You won't need to poke her."

"Thanks." I said. "But what do I do with this?" I knew the answer before I asked.

"Wear it." He took the cigar out of his mouth. He looked apologetic, the corner of his mouth tucking downward in a frown. "Your head. I mean his head." He pulled a rubber and black gorilla face out of his sack and handed it to me.

I held it up and stared at large rubber fangs painted white, an inside of a red mouth, a face blue-black with eyes empty slits beneath heavy-ridged brows.

"And he wants me to wear it?"

"For the show, Samantha. It was the best I could do."

So I put on the gorilla costume and climbed into Black Diamond's cage on top of the Colossus. I was hot, cooking within two minutes, looking for shade, roasting inside the costume. Sweat dripped down my arms and my back, wetting the fur of the costume, sticking it against my itchy skin. I panted through the mouth and fanned my arms up and down to circulate the still air around me.

Colonel Bob planned this deliberately, I thought. It was his idea of a joke. To teach me a lesson and to humiliate me. To remind me not to talk back. To follow orders. I was so mad I wanted to jump up and down and scream in rage at the line of people slowly filling into the Big Top, now pointing at me, eating candy and popcorn, laughing.

Jacko climbed on top of the Colossus, the tools in his wooden toolbox clanking against each other. Grinning, he poked his head around a corner of the cage and growled at me, his eyes wide in mock fright.

"Shut up," I snapped. "I'm burning up in all this hair."

"Sorry. Just humoring you. We're starting in a minute, and we'll get you inside of the tent and out of the sun. Where's Little Wolf?" He looked at the empty pedestal. "He'd better hurry up." He pulled a brass handle on the trap door and disappeared.

In the cage, soon I forgot all about Little Wolf because of my thirst. I stared through my bars, across the lot, heat rising in waves above the canvas, off the pavement. The red awning of Rosie's Pink Lemonade Stand peeked above a carousel of horses, carved mounts whirling kids around and around. Slivers of ice floated in the lemonade; frost coated the sides of the glass container. I looked at a water dish on the floor, empty, with an old cabbage leaf dried against the bottom, and started to yell to Jacko for a drink of water. But I had shouted too late.

With ringing bells and clanks, Harum's machinery shrieked and the Colossus lurched forward, a plume of steam skeining out of brass pipes. I lost my balance and sat down hard on the wooden floor, on my tailbone, and bounced through the entrance, the crowd buzzing and roaring as the Colossus entered the Big Top.

"Hey, look at the gorilla," someone yelled as the Colossus started down the hippodrome and around the ring. I squinted through the slits in my mask, sweat stinging my eyes, mad.

The bells and whistles deafened me. I clamped my hands against my ears, trying to block out the noise with the mask. Why hadn't I thought of earplugs? I thought, sliding across the cage's floor as the wagon turned a corner in front of some bleachers. I felt like throwing my hands up in the air and screaming in rage.

The driver wheeled the wagon to the side of the center ring and parked it. Now at the end of the tent, the wagon sat a few feet from the front row of bleachers, to one side, not blocking the spectators' view. Mercifully, the racket from the Colossus had stopped.

Finally, Samantha, you made the center ring, I thought, and snorted through rubber nostrils. You're a Starr. Some star.

A freckle-faced kid with red hair, clutching the string of a yellow balloon, swung his index finger at me like a weathervane. "Mom, that's no gorilla. That's a man in a monkey suit."

"You're right, honey. Daddy knows a gorilla when he sees one. Right Bill?" A woman with a purple scarf and a narrow face in a bright green dress lifted her eyes, smiling at her husband, a man with thick, hairy arms and a large stomach. She laughed.

He ripped a mouthful off his hot dog and didn't laugh. "Ah, shut up, Gertrude," he snarled.

The crowd would entertain me, help pass the time, I thought, sitting back on my haunches. I'd squat, watch people, imagine I was in a zoo, and not move too much. Although my costume still felt miserable, at least the sun wasn't pounding down on me and the Colossus wasn't moving and the machinery had stopped tooting and clanking. If I didn't move, the crowd would forget about me, and I could rest.

Colonel Bob danced around in the center ring, snapping his whip, waving his hat. His voice boomed above the yells and whistles of the crowd. "So sit back and enjoy Colonel Bob's Incredible Circus, Menagerie and Wild West Show—The Greatest Train and Wagon Show in the World, folks! Brought to you by special request as part of our gala tour of the Midwest."

He popped his whip toward Black Diamond's cage. "Now, direct your attention to the two cages. Rare and very dangerous gorillas from the Dark Continent." He spun and snapped his whip toward me, a smile flashing briefly across his face. "Watch them between acts."

I brushed back the shaggy wool hanging over my rubber slits and looked at Black Diamond's cage. I couldn't see her face. She sat, hunkered down in her corner, with her back to the crowd and the shouts. How did she control herself? I thought. Stay within herself against the frenzy outside her cage-the sounds, the smell, the colors, the motion. I'll act like Black Diamond, try to stay cool, ignore the circus, plan a revenge.

"Jump up and down for the folks, Sammy."

Outside my cage, Johnnie, a circus hand, was waving a stick at me and laughing. Behind him, the Marvelous Gomezes from Mexico were leading their Miracle Horses into the ring, two white geldings with flowing white manes and tails, silver saddles, red ostrich feathers and polished leather.

"You're kidding," I replied. "It's too hot."

He shrugged his shoulders. "You're supposed to jump up and down. Growl. Act like a gorilla. Kefe's orders."

Across the arena, Black Diamond roared, a scream of pain and anger. Another worker skipped backwards, a long stick in his hand. Black Diamond charged against the cage bars, smacking it with her chest, and the cage wobbled a bit. Shouts and screams crackled through the audience like static electricity.

"Like that, I guess." Johnnie said. "Only make-believe."

"Leave her alone," I screamed. "Who's jabbing her?"

"Kefe."

"He can't do that. Let me out of here." I hobbled for the cage door.

"Better not do that," Johnnie said. "The Colonel'll get mad at you and me." Quickly, he reached up and snapped the padlock shut.

Black Diamond roared again. The worker shook his stick in her face, danced a jig and spun around to face the audience, bowing. The crowd clapped and shouted. The band's trumpets and trombones blared out a fanfare, drums rolled, and the white horses danced around the ring.

I jumped at the cage door and shook it. "This isn't funny," I shouted. "Open it up!"

Johnnie shook his head, frowning. "Easy, Sammy. It's just a game. You come out of there and we both lose our jobs. I told Kefe I didn't want to shock anybody, but he said the Colonel wanted—"

"Some excitement. You and that big monkey, it is. This outfit needs more organization, it does. As bad as a pack of drunken redskins." A gravelly voice finished Johnnie's sentence.

Before I could swivel my mask around, a stick rattled through the bars and jabbed me in the ribs, hard. I gasped in pain and reached for my side.

"Now act like that other baboon. Hop around a bit! A little Irish jig for the folks."

I jumped for the stick, forgot the bars were there, and thumped my chest. I was looking down at Joe Kefe, a freckle-faced, strawberry blond Irishman from Dublin. He growled and shook his stick at me and laughed.

I was so mad that I jumped up and down and screamed, slapping my rubber feet against the floor of the cage. In answer, Black Diamond screamed and beat against her cage bars. Johnnie jumped backwards, holding his face in mock fright. The crowd clapped.

"Okay, that is a real live gorilla," the red-haired kid yelled.

I hollered again, and Black Diamond roared, so I sat down. When I get out of here, I'll kill Johnnie, I thought. And Colonel Bob. I really will. I'll burn them alive.

People gobbled popcorn and slurped ice drinks and smiled over fluffs of red and blue cotton candy. People pointed and laughed at me and made faces, twisting mouths and eyes into animal grimaces. Several times during the show, Johnnie darted at my cage in mock terror, but I didn't even move or complain. I just squatted down in the middle of my cage—Black Diamond's cage—and stared through the bars, focusing my anger, thinking mostly about myself, the circus, and Black Diamond.

Now I really know how it feels to sit in a cage like an animal, I thought. I had understood Black Diamond's pain and humiliation and her captivity and anger, dimly the way you grasp an idea but don't feel it. But I hadn't felt her misery the way I now did to the core of me. I cried in my mask. I felt ashamed of myself and of the circus and of my part in it: to take another creature, a living being, and treat it as a spectacle, a joke, a thing to laugh at and make money.

I argued again with two Samanthas—one standing on the outside of the cage looking in at the other hunkered down in her gorilla costume. I felt strange, my head swam, and I drifted. I didn't watch the acts that flowed before me, didn't hear the shouts of the audience, the music of the band, Colonel Bob's whip, Old Satan's roar, muffled through my mask.

Maybe animals don't understand and can't reason the way humans can, Samantha?

If we can reason. We should think about how they must feel and try to understand them.

Maybe they don't feel like we do?

They feel pain and anger and hunger. If they don't feel exactly like a human, is that any excuse for our treatment of them?

Aren't we more intelligent than they are?

We are more intelligent in some ways. But Black Diamond shows intelligence and can communicate. She uses a language. Suppose a mentally retarded child or a mute is born, the family certainly won't put the child in a cage, will they? And what is intelligence? How do you define it?

Aren't our morals better?

Look how we act. The wars. The murders. The way settlers treated the Indians.

124

Don't we make machines to work for us?

What is progress? Harum's Colossus? We make trains and light bulbs, but we've also made a Money Machine that grinds away at any cost.

Questions spun on into another and another like the whorls of a sticky spider's web. Sitting there in the cage, dazed, I couldn't answer all the questions exactly or completely. My mind didn't know all of the answers. But my heart felt and knew the answer: every animal is part of our village, our community, our large circus. Little Wolf. Jacko. Colonel Bob. The red-haired kid. Old Satan. Black Diamond. It's past time to treat one another, humans and animals, with respect and love and understanding, and not ridicule or shame them outside our village into the snow.

I stared through my bars at Black Diamond, her head down, her shoulders dropped, cornered in her cage—enduring Colonel Bob's Incredible Circus, Menagerie and Wild West Show—The Greatest Train and Wagon Show in the World. I knew some of her humiliation and endurance. If the Colonel treated Black Diamond this way—if all of us mistreated animals this way— then what about the Colonel's ideas of progress, advancing civilization? If America was that big family, that gigantic circus, then we needed to think how we put up the Big Top, how we designed the acts, how we treated the performers, ourselves.

Even then I didn't hate the Colonel. In a curious way, I still liked him in spite of showmanship, buckskin clothes, and silly speeches. I admired his striving to get ahead, to better himself and the circus. I too wanted to grow, to improve, to change myself. After all, hadn't I dreamed of starring under the Big Top?

Now I also realized it was wrong to make ourselves something more at the expense of others—people or animals. The Colonel couldn't really sense how Little Wolf felt about his ancestry, the way America had treated his people. He couldn't imagine Black Diamond's life in a cage. Like a small child who dresses his younger brothers and sisters up in old clothes, Colonel Bob thought of everyone as actors in his own private circus.

I don't remember how long I sat in the cage, but before the Deadwood coach charged into the ring in the Grand Finale, I had decided to leave the circus, the next night, after our final show. Even if it meant leaving my village and friends, my new ideas couldn't live with the way Colonel Bob ran his circus.

But I wasn't going to abandon Black Diamond, either. I only needed to figure out how to take Black Diamond with me, even to steal her. I didn't know where I was going or what I was going to do or how I was going to take care of a four-hundred-pound female gorilla. But I needed to save her from Colonel Bob's circus.

Plans

I dreamed again that night. A fire burned brightly, and dark shapes moved like wraiths before the flames, circling, squatting, speaking in grunts and signs. The fire warmed my face. I seemed to be sitting in a circle with someone, watching the flames blossom like roses, smelling animal smells and burning meat. I felt safe, protected by a large presence against the darkness beyond.

I awoke, lying in my bed, my neck sore and my mind fuzzy, trapped between my dream and the early morning sounds of sparrows chattering, their feet scrabbling on the wagon roof overhead, and the smells of bacon, toast, eggs, and coffee. I dressed in the tight space between my bed and the rear wall, putting on jeans, a white shirt, and pulling on a blue sweater against the sharp morning coolness.

I walked out into our wagon's main room, cramped with a small table and chairs, a soot-covered stove with a pipe snaking upward like a huge anaconda, beds, and camel-back trunks and crates. I had to squeeze myself out my door between a stack of costume boxes and feed buckets and the stove.

In the middle of the room, Jacko and Little Wolf were sitting at our small table, knees touching, heads close together, talking, steam from their coffee mugs eddying about their heads. Jacko poured a black stream of coffee from a battered blue-enameled pot and handed it to me, motioning me to sit on the edge of the bunk bed.

"Little Wolf's fired," Jacko said, a look of disgust on his face.

"Fired?" I asked.

"Kefe said he was tired of working with a drunken Indian. They argued."

I saw Kefe's ambitious eyes, heard his sarcasm, his wisecracks about Indians, smelled the sweet smell of the cough medicine on his breath. "But he's the one that's drinking! What did Colonel Bob say? Who's running the circus?"

"Honey, sometimes I wonder. The Colonel acts like he ain't heard about it. Anyway, Little Wolf wants to go back to Kansas."

Little Wolf was staring at his hands. His fingers, long and thin, trembled against the cup, shaking and spilling coffee over the rim when he drank. His black hair was uncombed and dirty. His eagle feather dangled at the side of his head, a comb with tufts of feathered teeth along a broken spine. Red rimmed his eyes.

His jaw tightened in anger. "I just can't take it anymore. Riding on the Colossus. White man's progress."

"Then I'm quitting, too," I said.

For a moment, no one spoke. Steam from my tin cup curled warmly against my face. Jacko rubbed the stubble of his beard, his rough hand scratching his face, like sandpaper. "Why?"

"Everything . . . Black Diamond . . . the way the Colonel treats . . ." Could I explain to them all of the ideas I had thought about in the cage?

Jacko poured himself another cup of coffee. "You don't need to explain. I understand. Where you fixing to go?"

"I don't know."

"When you going?"

"Tomorrow. After tonight's show," I said. "I'll sleep here tonight if you'll let me?"

"You betcha," Jacko said. His gold tooth flashed.

"Jacko, come with me." I suddenly blurted out my thoughts.

Jacko snipped off the end of a new cigar with his knife and rasped a match against the table, spurting blue flame between his fingers. He puffed on the cigar, exhaling blue smoke, watching smoke from the match curl upward, his dark face thoughtful.

"White folks wouldn't like it. An Indian and black man traveling together with a white girl. They'd ask too many questions. Cause problems. It's okay here, in the circus. Among friends," Jacko said. He flicked the ash of his cigar. "But not out there." His voice sounded bitter, like wind through corn stalks, brown and dry.

He was right of course. A black man and Indian didn't travel with a white girl, even as friends in America.

"If you don't mind me asking, what you gonna do, Samantha?" He called me that when he was being serious, when he recognized me as an adult. He knitted the wrinkles of his forehead together, slowly, thoughtfully, his thick, white eyebrows two heavy caterpillars.

I should have asked myself that question and many others. I hadn't thought of what I wanted to do, where I was going, how I was going to live. I was running away from what I didn't want to do anymore, away from my disappointment and from what the circus represented.

"I'm not staying anymore."

Jacko held up his hand, a light, chocolate-color on the palm, crisscrossed with small, white scars. "I understand, and I'm not trying to talk you into staying. Samantha, I've been watching you around that gorilla. Been thinking to myself. You need to educate yourself. Go to school and make something of yourself."

"With what?"

The circus is a job, but its wages are excitement and adventure and travel, not silver dollars or five-dollar gold pieces. I slept on my narrow cot, ate my share of ham and beans in the cook tent, and squirreled away a few dollars in an old Prince Albert tobacco can, tucked away with my favorite science books in my battered trunk. I owned about what most circus people owned: not much—a few odds and ends. Really, a lot of circus people can't afford to run away from a circus, even if they want to, because poor circus pay cages them in the Big Top, stops them from leaving, running off to find another job.

Jacko scraped his chair back, away from the table, and stood up. He walked over to his bed, shoved it away from the wall, and lowered himself carefully on his hands and knees in the corner of the room, using the bed and wall to brace himself, his arms and hands hidden by his back. Then, slowly he stood up with a small, red metal box. In the corner, a dark hole winked at us from a spot between the floor and the wall.

"Here," Jacko said, turning the box upside down on the table. Wadded dollars and coins funneled upwards into a small pyramid. A gold eagle gleamed between Morgan silver dollars. "Your traveling money."

"You mean your retirement money," I said. "You can't do that and I won't take it." How many years had he hoarded the money and saved it, with what dreams of retirement? I wondered.

Jacko grinned, the creases on his face wrinkling upward. "Oh, I'm not giving it to you," he said. "I'm managing it for you—for us." He reached across the table and patted Little Wolf on the shoulder. "For all of us."

I was astounded. "You'd quit the circus?"

Jacko sat down, leaned back in his chair, and then lowered his face close to the pile of money, studying it closely, as if he had just unearthed a buried treasure. Then, he lifted his face and looked at me and smiled. "Circus is family. And we's family."

I felt like crying. With the tip of my finger, I pushed off the top of the pile a five-dollar bill, crinkled and worn smooth and shiny in the creases, and said, "Thanks."

"Now, what you . . . we gonna do with that gorilla, Samantha?" Jacko asked.

"I don't know."

Little Wolf pushed the brown sack across the table toward Jacko, around the coins and dollar bills. "Throw that away. Take the gorilla with us." His pupils widened, then narrowed into slits.

"That's stealing," I said, my voice uncertain. He reminded me of an old circus wolf too long caged, dangerous, waiting to lash out.

His anger nipped me. His eyes challenged me. "The white man stole her from her land."

Jacko held up his hand between us like a thick, weather-stained oak wedge. "Okay, okay. You're both right. Samantha, go eat some breakfast. Cookie's got grits and bacon. Little Wolf and I will think about this, talk over our gorilla problem."

Outside, the sunlight now bounced harshly off concrete buildings, a white heat. The air pressed against me as if I'd opened a hot oven. The smell of fried potatoes and cooked cabbage and sour garbage drifted heavily in the air, mixing with asphalt and tar. In the street, a delivery man in a blue uniform with sweat stains under his arms banged a metal keg out of the rear of a beer wagon and shoved it through saloon doors. A dapple-gray horse stood in harness, head down, balanced on three legs and a cocked hind one, asleep in the heat.

Instead of going to breakfast, I walked over to say good morning to Black Diamond. Every day, I usually gave her leftovers I'd scrounged up from the cook tent—a carrot or piece of celery. The menagerie tent hung in shadows from the tall buildings, dew-drenched, its entrance open, the canvas draping like a shroud. Old Satan was resting in his cage, awake, his tail flopping back and forth, thumping hollow sounds against the wooden floor of his cage. A raccoon was lying on a log, asleep on his stomach, his legs splayed over the sides.

Black Diamond was waiting for me, sitting near the bars of her small cage. Harum's Colossus was parked in front of her cage, pushed there after the show, in case of rain. She had to listen to the mechanical monstrosity during the performance, and then she had to sleep next to it.

"Could I buy you?" I said, thinking out loud, seeing the pile of Jacko's money on the table, yet knowing how foolish that sounded.

"Wraagh." Black Diamond curled her arms around her chest and stared. She looked uncomfortable, cramped in the old cage, its floor littered with lettuce leaves.

"You need some housecleaning," I said, my nose wrinkling at her squalid stench. "And some more space."

"Wraagh," she sounded.

"But I can't stay. I just don't believe what the circus stands for anymore," I said as I slid half an apple through the bars.

Black Diamond didn't move. She just stared at me, her eyes dark under her thick brows, as if she knew what I was going to say—that I intended to take her with me.

"You need me, don't you? We're still friends," I muttered. "You stood up for me in the warehouse."

Then, I started to cry, not loudly, but softly, the tears running down my face. "I can't leave you with Colonel Bob's show. I won't," I said, wiping my nose with the back of my sleeve. "I'll talk to . . ."

Then, I heard Colonel Bob's voice, loud, in his best salesman's pitch, just before he stepped through the tent opening. I ducked down, dropped on my hands and knees and crawled behind two wooden barrels beside Black Diamond's cage. I knelt down, my face pressed against the rough wood, my eyes staring through the slit between the barrels.

131

Four legs from the waist down, two in white buckskin and two in a shiny, sleek, black material, filled the gap in the barrels. Colonel Bob's brown boots were scuffed, a clump of dried mud on the toe of one of them. The other pair of black boots gleamed in the trampled grass, polished, dark leather mirrors of care and elegance.

"And how much do you want for it?" The speaker asked the question carefully, said the simple words smoothly, enunciated the tones precisely, with concern yet with a certain distance. A coldness, like that in a darkened funeral parlor, frosted the words. I felt a chill and shivered.

"Now that depends on the conditions of sale," Colonel Bob replied eagerly, excitedly. "What's your offer?"

"It's not in the best of condition," the voice replied, a touch of pity behind the silkiness, as if the speaker weren't blaming Colonel Bob for the condition of Harum's Colossus.

"True, Professor Ripton," replied the Colonel, "but it wouldn't take much to . . . shall we say, to improve it."

"I'll give you fifty dollars for it." The voice now sounded resigned, as if the speaker were favoring the Colonel with an offer that was obviously much too high, an offer that was more of a gift than a bid.

Fifty dollars for Harum's Colossus? I held my hand to my mouth, almost laughing out loud at the thought of Colonel Bob's mechanical contraption selling for fifty dollars. Hadn't he planned to make millions with his Colossus?

"Nope," the Colonel replied, his voice firm. "Seventy-five dollars or no deal."

Seventy-five dollars? How could he sell it for seventy-five dollars? He must have paid Harum hundreds of dollars.

"My good Colonel," the voice said smoothly again, drawing out the syllables, softening them, "This fine specimen will require numerous alterations. Many exhibits must pass before I regain my initial capital investment. As it is, it is worthless to me." A suggestion of disinterest crept into his voice.

Alterations? True, he could tone down the whistles and bells. I almost stood up to see the Colonel's face. He was meeting someone who also understood Progress with a capital P, I thought, with a smirk on my face.

"Well, I guess I see your point, Professor Ripton. Winter's coming on." The Colonel's voice sounded too eager. He'd sensed the warning, the threat in Ripton's offer, and understood that he might lose a customer if he pushed too hard. "Say sixty-five dollars then."

"I'm delighted that you are reconsidering, Colonel," Professor Ripton said. "For sixty dollars—in gold—I will duly note your contributions and former ownership in the advertisements of the exhibit." After a slight paused, coins clanked together in metallic intervals.

"You're very persuasive, today, Professor." Colonel Bob's voice now sounded pleased, satisfaction ringing in it like the tinkle of a brass cash register. "Done."

"I assume the cage goes with the exhibit."

Colonel Bob coughed in his hand. "Well, I . . . no, that will cost five dollars more. Those are solid steel bars. And you can hardly do without it."

The cage? I felt a slight chill crawl down my back.

"True, but you do not need it now. Four dollars seems an appropriate price." The Professor slid his words out, carefully, drawing them out, like a cardsharp slowly turning over four aces.

"Done."

"Excellent." The boots moved closer together and coins clanked. "I will pick it up tomorrow. Your gorilla will make a fine addition to Professor Ripton's Traveling Museum."

I was stunned, my knees weak, my arms shaking. I felt dizzy, like I had been spinning too much in a barrel trick in the center ring.

"Think and think quickly, Samantha," I said.

My head swirled. Colonel Bob had sold Black Diamond, and I hadn't said anything. For sixty dollars. Jacko's money. Of course. I'd offer Colonel Bob more and buy her back. No, he'd already sold her. I'd use Jacko's money to buy her from the Professor.

I jumped up from behind the barrels, but the tent was empty, except for a heavy silence.

An Offer

I found Colonel Bob in a shadow beside his trailer, beneath the painting of the huge gorilla smashing through trees, clutching a piece of raw meat, its face twisted in a nightmare of hate and anger. For a moment the Colonel looked startled, his eyes widening, then just annoyed when I walked up to him.

I didn't hesitate, but I controlled the shake and anger in my voice. "I want to buy Black Diamond." I looked straight into his blue eyes, dark spots under the brim of his white hat. He stared back at me, started to say something, blinked, then looked away.

"He's not for sale," he said, turning to go, dismissing me with a short wave of his hand.

I grabbed his forearm. Beneath the slick and grimy buckskin, his wrist and arm felt bony, like a skeleton. He stared down at my hand, and then at me, the wrinkled skin tightening over his jaw. Up close, he looked like an old man, not a Wild West hero, tired, worried, his skin gray beneath a light veil of powder, tiny red veins crawling along the side of his nose. He smelled of stale tobacco and sour whiskey and dried sweat.

"Black Diamond is a *she*. A *she*," I replied, speaking slowly and emphasizing the words. "You've never understood that."

Colonel Bob brushed at my hand with one of his fringed gloves as if he were swatting a horsefly. "Please," he said.

I let go of his arm. For an instant, standing beneath the reds and greens and yellows and painted hippos and giraffes illustrating his circus, he reminded me of a clown dressed as a shabby cowboy.

"I want to buy Black Diamond," I repeated, emphasizing each word.

Colonel Bob laughed, a short barking snarl. "Ha. Ha. With what?"

"I'll give you a hundred dollars for her." Did the pile of coins and paper even total a hundred dollars?

Interest and greed slipped across his face and his eyes narrowed. "How'd you know he was for sale?"

I wanted to look down at my feet, but I didn't. "I overheard you in the menagerie tent with the Professor." I stared back at him.

"A spy, huh. Probably German." He shook his head in disgust and spat on the ground. "Then you know I've already sold him. The cage, too. Now go on back to work or . . . " He turned to walk away.

"Wait," I said. He turned back, his shoulders slumping, the shadow from the wagon cutting through the middle of him like a black saber. "Please. Why did you sell her?"

His face dropped. "I didn't want to . . . I mean," one hand wiped the back of his neck. He sounded like he wanted to cry. "Money. Harum Scarum tricked me with all of that walnut on the Colossus. Expenses. I could have talked to The Wizard." He looked across the lot. Two workmen, laughing and talking, were stepping out of the cook tent. Bennie, a skinny sword swallower who stood on stilts and doubled as the World's Tallest Man, splashed a pail of water in the dust.

Colonel Bob sounded distracted, continuing as if he were searching in the grass for a lost nickel. "Everything's just too expensive. Feed. Wages. We're not making enough. Too expensive. More than I planned." His words trailed off, lost someplace, confused in his thoughts.

Suddenly, I wasn't angry anymore. Just sad, I guess. And disappointed. Now, the Colonel wasn't the glorious Wild West hero who'd ridden with Buffalo Bill and toured with Annie Oakley. He was defeated, his dreams lost, vanishing before him, just as the romanticism of his past was slipping away like tired ghosts, wanting rest. I wondered where he would go, and I saw a tired old man thumbing through *Triumphs and Struggles* or listening to the metallic voice of The Wizard of Menlo on his phonograph in a shabby house someplace, on the edge of some shabbier Western town, weathering away in sun and snow, locked in tumbleweeds and tall Johnson grass.

He was still talking, to no one in particular now, as if I weren't standing beside him. "I just needed the money. You can't progress without money. But progress brings money, doesn't it? Winter's coming on. Maybe if I cut to the bare bone. Drop the dog act. Then I can still . . ." He stopped.

Wasn't a circus family? Didn't we need to help each other? If I could have saved him and his wild west show, I would have tried. But I couldn't hold up the whole Big Top, stop the ropes from fraying around us. I needed to save what I could.

"They fired Little Wolf," I said.

He acted as if he hadn't heard me.

"They fired Little Wolf."

His face flinched. "Something about drinking, wasn't it? No, that's not right! Fired you say? Who did? I'm still running this show." He smacked a heavy fist into his palm and threw out his chest. "Larger! That's it! We'll expand. Get two dog acts instead of one."

His eyes narrowed. Smiling strangely, he looked above my head, as if he had suddenly noticed someone. I turned around quickly.

On the canvas painting of the gorilla and trees, a hunter in buckskins crouched, his hat off, pointing two six-shooters at the gorilla. A flap of heart-shaped canvas hung from the hunter's chest.

"That's not right," he said.

"No, it's not." I turned back to him. "There's something else. Where's the Professor?" I asked.

"What professor?"

"You know. The Professor."

The Colonel looked at me, wearily. "Someplace on Fifty-fourth Street."

That someplace on Fifty-fourth street was a store between a pawnshop filled with ragged clothes, used bicycles, and rusty tools and a pool hall, its window covered with beer signs and dead flies. Across a door, a sign in black letters edged in gold read:

PROFESSOR RIPTON'S
TRAVELING ANIMAL EXHIBITS
AND OTHER MARVELS

When I pushed in the door, Professor Ripton was perched at his desk, like a vulture, his black tuxedo hanging like wings, writing on a green sheet of paper. A doorbell on a cord jangled, and he looked up.

He smiled, cocking his head, before he fluttered down from a distant limb. "May I help you, young lady?" A bouquet of red carnations in a blue vase stood next to a golden cigar box.

I stepped closer. Professor Ripton wore a black bow tie and a starched shirt, the collar stiff against his thin, white neck. His face was v-shaped, with the chin the bottom of the v, indented as if someone had chipped a piece out of marble. Eyes like chips of broken violet glass glimmered beneath gold-framed glasses. His nose wrinkled as if he were smelling a bad odor, and he looked me up and down.

"I'm from the circus." I wondered if he hadn't guessed that when I had walked in, from my clothes.

"Colonel Bob's enterprise, I presume," he said. He capped his fountain pen, a heavy gold tube, and arranged it precisely in front of his green paper.

"Yes, sir," I replied. "I work in the menagerie."

Thin eyebrows tightened over narrow eyes. "The one with the marvelous specimen of the Western gorilla. In poor condition though."

Where was his animal exhibit? I wondered, glancing around the room. Except for his mahogany desk and a red, leather couch against the wall, under a gold plaque with engraved lettering, his room was empty, hollow, and cool, and reminded me of a tomb, one of those elegant marble ones with colonnaded entrances.

"And you're here to protect her?" he asked bluntly, tipping his hands together into a small tent.

"I . . . you know me?"

"Aren't you the girl who fought with the boys in front of the animals?" he asked, smiling a thin, tight line.

Then I remembered. Professor Ripton, a black shadow in the background, had walked behind the bullies that first day.

He guessed my next thought, even before I formed it myself. "No, I wasn't connected to them. Crude really. No control or art. Certainly animalistic."

"What is it that you do?" I asked.

He pointed toward the window. "Exhibit animals and other marvels. Nature's oddities."

"But I don't see any."

"Of course you don't. My company displays them elsewhere. The exhibit travels in large cities. I merely procure the, ah, curiosities, shall we say." He smiled with satisfaction and glanced behind him at a walnut-stained door with a gold knob.

"You would care to see some of our stored curiosities? Being an exhibitor of sorts yourself." Behind the door, the room was dark and cool and musty smelling. Professor Ripton struck a thick-head match, a yellow flame of foul sulphur. Boxes and crates and shapes wavered in the dark beyond the pool of light.

"A prized possession," he said, pointing toward a dark form. "Rare really, after the likes of Colonel Bob almost exterminated them."

Between two large crates, a stuffed buffalo seemed to leap out of the shadows at me, glass eyes reflecting the flickering match light, head and horns lowered.

Professor Ripton struck another match. "See the snow owl. Our taxidermist preserved it beautifully in its winter plumage. Another rarity. I located the creature in a menagerie."

"Alive?" I asked, feeling a cold draft.

"Of course. Our best specimens are. Initially." He stepped forward and struck another match and waited for it to flare, throwing a splash of yellow over boxes and forms. "But life's too expensive and inefficient. Why pay for the upkeep when we may keep the specimen forever?" He coughed in his hand, lightly. "Would you like to see, ah, some of our more unusual exhibits? Nature's anatomical mistakes. Animal—and human?"

I was shaking inside, and I wanted to run, shouting for help. I had seen and heard enough to know what Professor Ripton did with his exhibits, enough to know what he intended to do with Black Diamond.

The match went out. "I would like to buy Black Diamond back from you," I said in the darkness.

"A black diamond. We don't deal in gems. Only in—"

"Colonel Bob's gorilla. The one you bought from him. That's her name."

"I'm terribly sorry," he said, his words emotionless in the dark, steady and controlled. "But I have a major museum in New York who has already contracted to display the gorilla. We also supply schools." He sounded proud of himself.

"You're going to kill her," I said, keeping my voice level, holding my fright and anger in a tiny cage someplace in my mind.

He paused for a moment. "You speak too crudely. I prefer nicer words. Euthanasia or preservation. To memorialize."

I didn't want to anger him. "I will pay you sixty-five dollars."

"The gorilla is worth much more than that."

"One hundred." How could I ever get a hundred dollars? I wondered.

In the darkness, his voice was the final latching of the tomb door, a shutting out of hope by an undertaker of death. "I'm so terribly sorry, my dear. But my gorilla is not for sale. Now, let me escort you out of this dark place. I must complete my paper work."

So I stood outside of his door, staring at old tools and baskets and rusty guns in the pawnshop and listening to droning voices from the saloon, hurting, trying to think of how to save Black Diamond. What could I do? I thought. Even if Jacko had enough money and would loan it to me, Professor Ripton wouldn't sell Black Diamond. They were going to kill, and murder her, and mount her in a glass showcase for a New York museum.

I started to cry. I almost ran then, away from St. Louis, toward the railroad yards, to jump a freight train to anywhere, to escape myself, to forget my friends in boxcars and hardships. But I didn't. Instead, I became very angry, not fist-throwing angry, but cold and calculating, the kind of anger that doesn't care for the consequences, that will dare any risk.

I turned back toward the circus. I was going to steal Black Diamond and let someone try and stop me.

Decisions

After I left Professor Ripton's Traveling Animal Exhibits and Other Marvels, I wandered around, looking in store windows, devising different ways to steal Black Diamond. I knew stealing was wrong, but I was so frustrated I didn't even debate the rightness or wrongness of taking her. I didn't care. I just knew that somehow I wouldn't let Professor Ripton get her.

I imagined different schemes to take Black Diamond, but none of them, even the simplest, seemed possible, by myself. How could a fifteen-year-old girl steal a gorilla and vanish in St. Louis without being caught?

"I can't. I can't do it," I said out loud.

But then I would see Black Diamond in Professor Ripton's horrible storage room and I try to think of another idea to help her. The more I wandered around in the cage of my mind the more frustrated and angry and frightened I became.

At last, a black vulture of resignation fluttered down and perched on my shoulder to peck at my heart. I wanted to quit, to give up. I almost did, I almost ran away, but I remembered that my idea of a circus had changed and instead of a hiding place it could still mean family. So I brushed at the vulture, made it lift its heavy head and wings a bit, and walked back to the Big Top, to our wagon, feeling trapped but not totally defeated. Yet.

"Why didn't you come back sooner?" Jacko asked. He was sitting on the edge of his bed, his toolbox at his feet. Standing in front of the mirror, Little Wolf was painting red and black stripes across his cheeks.

Jacko frowned at me. "Didn't I tell you Little Wolf and I'd talk about *our gorilla problems*? Where you been?"

I explained to him about my visit to Professor Ripton, about his warehouse of horrors.

Jacko's eyebrows shot up, anger flaring across his face. Little Wolf smeared too much red paint across his chin, muttered something to himself, and then wiped it off with a towel.

"We're taking her with us," Little Wolf said, putting on his headdress with white eagle feathers.

"But I thought Bill fired you?"

"He did, but he's not running the show yet."

"Where are we going?" I asked. The police would arrest all of us for stealing, I thought. A black man, an Indian in war paint, a gorilla, and a foolish girl.

"To Kansas." His eyes flicked over me briefly. "To my ranch." His voice was determined, resolved, under control again.

I remembered the Victorian house with the odd tower facing the flat buttes and empty horizon, the strange sense of a wolf lurking, watching just beyond my vision, as if it were a guardian, the spirit of a free place, waiting now for us to come home.

"How will we—"

Jacko held up a large, square hand, his calluses like rough pebbles across his palm and fingers. "Honey, don't you worry about no details, now. These two old circus freaks know a few tricks or two yet. Just get into your monkey suit and don't worry." Jacko picked up his toolbox and opened the wagon door for Little Wolf. "See you on the Colossus."

I picked the gorilla suit off my bed, excited, nervous, filled with hope and unanswered questions, questions I had avoided earlier but I now needed to ask myself. I pushed my feet down into the legs of the costume, hurrying to get dressed for the grand spectacle, my mind racing.

It is wrong to steal, isn't it, Samantha Starr? The state of Missouri didn't mince any words about thieves. The Big House was filled with prisoners who had stolen horses and cattle, worth much less than Black Diamond. If we took Black Diamond, we were breaking the law. We would be thieves, they would arrest us, and we'd go to prison.

Fine, Samantha. But killing an intelligent and innocent being who could reason was wrong. Professor Ripton was going to kill Black Diamond for his exhibits, for a few lousy bucks. She wasn't my property, but she was my friend, family really, and I wasn't about to let her die. I'd go to jail first.

I put on my itchy monkey face and shuffled out the wagon door toward the Colossus. Little Wolf, dressed in full battle gear, rifle in hand, was waiting for me. He helped me into the cage and shut the door and climbed up on his pedestal.

As the door clanged behind me, I had a vision of myself in prison, locked away with other thieves and robbers, forgotten in some tiny cellblock, in an airless box with metal beds riveted to the wall and a slot for feeding. I wondered if the judge would send Little Wolf and Jacko to the same prison. Probably not. Didn't they send girls to a different place, someplace easier? Maybe I'd go to a reformatory, one of those ivy-covered brick buildings with wire-covered windows, surrounded by barbed-wire fences. And where would they send Black Diamond? Back to Professor Ripton?

The Colossus's whistles shrieked and gears turned and steam hissed and bells gonged. "Don't lock the door," I said to Little Wolf above the noise. Suddenly afraid, I sensed something, indescribable, odd, felt a coldness press toward my face, my eyes, as if a cold finger were measuring and dropping heavy pennies against my eyelids. I shuddered at the image.

He laughed, snapped the padlock shut, and hung the keys on a nail beside one of the pipes. I was ready for the final circus performance of my life.

Escape

The Colossus lurched forward into the Big Top, bells clanging and steam whistles tooting.

Boots, a tattooed ticket-taker, smiled and waved a brawny arm at me as the Colossus rolled through the entryway. Inside, the band blared a John Philip Sousa march, horns blowing, drums rattling, and spectators jostled each other, a jumble of colors and faces—an old man in a heavy white beard and a blue cap, a thin woman waving a small American flag, a small boy in overalls and a girl in a red dress holding hands, laughing. Fresh sawdust silted the ground like white sand. Overhead, the canvas looked like a giant pinwheel with blue and red and white canvas stripes swirling away from the center tent pole.

This may be your last chance ever to be a circus star, so enjoy it, Samantha, I said to myself, settling back in my cage, not even pretending to act like a gorilla. I couldn't concentrate, couldn't enjoy the circus unfolding before me like a child's coloring book. I could sit and think only of stealing Black Diamond and of freedom on a windswept prairie in Kansas with Jacko and Little Wolf—or of prison, in a girls' reformatory, by myself, staring through mesh windows at my last freedom.

"Come on. Jump up and down for the crowd," Kefe said. Acting, he shook his stick at me menacingly.

"Go drop dead," I stared at him.

"Still in a bad mood, are we?" He shrugged his shoulders, turned, and watched the center ring. "Every day, you get more and more like the real thing, Sammy."

In the center ring, Colonel Bob waved his hat at the crowd and cracked his bullwhip at the clowns.

A couple of joeys had started their fireman's gag. A fat clown in a frizzy red wig, dressed as a large woman in a bright green housecoat, jumped up and down, trying to attract the attention of another clown, a skinny cop, in a blue overcoat with white buttons the size of dinner plates and a tall black hat, rounded like an upside-down jar, who was idly rocking back and forth on his heels. The woman hopped up and down, housecoat flapping, tugging at the cop's coat, pointing at a small pink cardboard house. With his head and shoulders poked out of the second-story window, Joey the Midget, his face framed in a baby's bonnet, waved a huge wooden baby pacifier and wailed, red-faced.

Beneath him, white clouds of smoke from dry ice billowed upward.

"Fire, fire," screamed the mother, tugging at the cop's coat.

Confused, the cop turned and scanned the horizon, both elbows at his side, like the wings of a giant crow, looking in the stands, ignoring the house behind him. Flames of yellow and orange crepe streamers flapped out of the windows, and the baby screamed more loudly.

The clown in the housecoat pulled the cop around by his coat, gesturing frenetically at the flames. Finally, the cop saw the burning house, heard the screams. "The fire department. The fire department. Call the fire department. Call the cops. Call me," the cop yelled, running in circles around the burning house. After fumbling around with their gear, two firemen charged in, in red underwear, carrying huge, blue buckets, sloshing water as they ran, falling over each other.

"Fire! Fire!" the mother screamed.

I had forgotten my problems and was enjoying the show, when I smelled a hot burning, a metal odor. Funny, I thought, the joeys have added some chemical for realism, for the acrid smell of fire.

Then yellow smoke, black on the edges, rolled in front of my cage, like a ring of poisonous mushrooms.

144

"A fire. Fire!" A worker ran past my cage, pointing toward me, toward Colonel Bob in the center ring. The crowd roared in laughter.

A fire? I asked dully, confused, standing up. A couple of clowns were sloshing buckets of water and confetti at each other, and now two clowns struggled to lean an orange ladder against the side of the cardboard house.

Then I looked across the hippodrome at the animal cages. Instead of lying down asleep, Old Satan was stalking back and forth, his tail switching, his ears pulled tightly against his head. The raccoons were darting up and down their log, a blur of white and black, chattering.

Black Diamond was sitting up, hands gripping the bars of her cage, facing me. "Wraagh!" Her scream pierced the laughter of the crowd.

Hair on the back of my neck jumped. Another billow of smoke rolled across the ring, blocking the clowns from view and floating into my cage. Someone screamed. In the audience, a few people jumped to their feet, pointing in my direction. Others were laughing and clapping at the clowns. A thin woman clutching a child crawled under a yellow barricade and ran toward the single exit, her head twisted backwards. Now, Colonel Bob was yelling something through a megaphone, waving it toward the crowd, pointing at the exit.

Fire. There is a fire. I thought, dully. I had to get out of the cage.

Suddenly, Bill the ringmaster stood before me, his face sweat-streaked, his eyes wide, in front of the cage. "Get out, Sammy," he yelled, pointing. "The Colossus caught fire. Run for it." He waddled off toward the exit, his coattails flapping.

I bolted for the cage door, hit it with my hands and chest, and sat down, the wind knocked out of me. For a moment, choking in the smoke, I was stunned.

Locked. The lock was jammed. I was locked in the cage.

I stood up, and, putting both hands on the cage bars, shook the door and screamed.

"Let me out!"

Now the cage floor felt hot through the padded feet, and my eyes stung with sweat.

The keys, I thought, looking through the bars. Get the keys and unlock the door. I pressed my face to the bars, trying to remember where Little Wolf had put them.

The ring of keys hung from the nail. I reached for them. Too far. I couldn't reach them. Panicked now, I jammed my arm through the bars and strained toward the keys, the bars hurting my shoulder and neck.

Someone ran by the cage, screaming.

I held my breath and stretched until I couldn't feel my shoulder or neck. The tips of my fingers brushed the keys; they jiggled on the nail slightly, but I couldn't reach them.

A stick! I need a stick. Anything!

Frantic, I dropped to the floor, looking for a stick, for something to push through the bars to lift the keys off the nail. Gasping for breath, I crawled and scrambled around the inside of the cage, sweeping my hands across the floor. The floor was empty.

Trapped!

Then I seemed to be another person standing outside the cage, watching a gorilla slowly pull herself up and stumble across the cage toward the door. At the door, I tripped over my gorilla feet and fell. Smoke choked me, and heat smothered me, like an animal pressing its weight against me, curling its heat fingers to strangle me. I couldn't breathe. Before me, a dark tunnel shaped like a circus ring filled with swirling horses spun around and around, and I was galloping on a black horse toward the center of a dark spot ringed with fire.

Suddenly, I was jerked to my feet.

"Get the mask off!" The voice was distant. I didn't care now. I was riding toward the center ring.

Then my lungs seemed to explode with cooler air. I gasped for breath, and the dark spot wavered and blurred into a face. Little Wolf stood before me, his knife in his hand.

"Don't move." He grabbed my gorilla costume, pulled it away from my body, stroked downward—once, twice, three times. My costume fell away in strips, and I was standing in my underwear, almost naked, wet with sweat, my skin cool against the smoke and heat. I was out of the cage. Behind me, flames crackled and a solid wall of heat clawed us.

I turned and looked at the Colossus. Flames prowled along the floor of my cage, licking through the bars, and black smoke roiled upward, an oily smudge rising, hiding metal pipes and whistles. On the side of the wagon, part of Colonel Bob's face and beard stared at me from the charred oval, blistered and darkened with the heat.

"Where's Jacko?" I yelled. "We can't leave Jacko."

"The animals," Little Wolf said, coughing. Around the Colossus, more flames lapped in the sawdust, greedily, bright tongues of red and orange. People were screaming and running through the smoke, dim figures. A boy holding a stuffed bear ran into Little Wolf, crying. Little Wolf reached down and picked him up.

Cursing, a heavy set man in a dark suit, wearing glasses with one lens, charged out of the smoke and bumped into Little Wolf. He pulled the boy away from Little Wolf. Little Wolf grabbed the man by the arm, tearing his coat sleeve.

So this is the end, I thought, unable to move, petrified, my body shaking, my mind numb, far away. *I'm going to die here.*

""Wraagh!" Black Diamond's roar of pain pierced me.

"This way. Before the tent falls." Little Wolf pulled on the man's arm. "Samantha, follow me." He disappeared into the smoke, leading the man.

"Wraaaagh!"

Black Diamond was calling me, I thought. She would die. Burn to death. In her cage.

I ran toward the sound, coughing, holding my hand to my mouth, keeping my head down closer to the ground. Old Satan roared. Men were yelling and women screaming. Fire popped and crackled around me, bright flashes of flame in the wooden bleachers.

"Wraaaagh!" Her howl was desperate now.

The heavy stench of burning canvas washed over me as I ran through the center ring, around a couple of green barrels. Hurry. Hurry before the tent falls, I thought, coughing. I tripped over something hard and sprawled, hitting my head, grinding my face in the sawdust.

I felt stunned, dizzy. I knew I had to stand up, to run, but my body wouldn't respond and my mind drifted, aware of the sights and sounds and smell of the fire. I don't know how long I lay there—a few seconds or a few minutes—before I rolled over and stared up at the top of the tent, the point where ropes and wires whorled to the center pole like a giant spider's web. The center pole, I thought lazily, watching fire scamper like red spiders along ropes toward the canvas. The Big Top. The center of the circus.

"Wraagh." The voice was distant pleading, an echo from my past, my memory, dreams. Someone talking to me around a campfire, sharing warmth and food. I was dreaming, not dreaming.

Wake up, Samantha. Your friend is calling you. Needs you. Stand up.

Crack!

Above me, hazy in the smoke, the center pole shivered and swayed, snapping guy wires, the top of the canvas dropping down, sagging, a thick curtain ready to drop, burying all of us. I curled into a ball, a tiny fetus, fascinated, still unable to move.

Boom!

Ropes pulled away, cutting through the air, whipping like snakes, sparking with flames. The center pole jerked as if alive, held a moment, teetered, with folds of canvas draped around it, a dark obscene toadstool of death, and then toppled, axing downward over me.

One frayed rope lashed my legs, stinging them. The center pole smashed into the ground beside me, twenty feet away, spraying dirt and sawdust. The canvas sagged over me, the bowels of some gigantic fish, suspended above the ground, held in place by steel cables.

"Wraagh!"

"Help! Someone help me!"

I stood up, my face wet with sweat.

"Wraagh!"

"Get this thing off my legs!"

I turned toward the sound of the human voice and ran along the pole, choking in the smoke, jumping ropes and cables, tripping over a body in a suit, sprawled on the ground.

"Help!" The voice was now frantic.

I nearly bumped into Old Satan's cage. There, pinned by his legs beneath the crumpled wagon, his upper body twisted around, lay Colonel Bob. Above him, the top of the center pole had struck the roof of Old Satan's wagon, caving the roof in, popping its yellow wheels off, sending them spinning away like huge buttons. The door hung open, and the cage was empty.

Pain and shock contorted Colonel Bob's face. "Stupid of me. Trying to free that worthless cat. Pull me out of here."

"Wraagh!"

"Hurry up!"

I turned toward Black Diamond, then back to Colonel Bob, hearing the crackle and pop of fire, knowing it was spreading beneath the canvas.

Hurry, I said to myself. Hurry up. You still have time.

Trying to lift the edge of the wagon off Colonel Bob's legs, I pulled until my arms hurt, the muscles straining in my back and legs. But I couldn't move it, not even budge the wagon away from his legs.

"Get that pole," he shouted, his voice high and panic-stricken, pointing at a pole the trapeze team used to balance themselves. He coughed and blood edged the corners of his mouth. Smoke billowed, swirled around us, and the heat pressed against me, burning, suffocating, sucking my breath from me. I gasped for air as a furnace of canvas and ropes and sawdust and wooden bleachers roared and snapped behind me.

"Wraagh!" Black Diamond's call was a plea too.

I'll faint. I can't drag the pole wagon. I'm not strong enough to lift it. I don't weigh enough.

The tent flaming around me, I dropped to my hands and knees in the sawdust. "I'll come back," I said to him. His eyes stared at me, flooded with desperation and horror. I turned to go. I didn't want to look at him again and I didn't. I felt poisoned inside, leaving him.

"Samantha! Girl! Don't leave me! Please."

As I crawled away, I kept my head as low to the ground as I could, my face inches away from the sawdust. I crawled on my hands and knees, my lungs gasping for air.

Somehow I found my way beneath the downed canvas, through the twisted ropes and over the broken center pole. As I thought my lungs would burst, I crawled through a small space, into a pocket of cooler air, like a white tunnel, propped up by part of the pole. The scorching heat stopped, the smoke was less dense, and I could breath easier. The Big Top had collapsed here too, but not completely. Somehow the poles and ropes and guy wires at this end of the tent still kept the canvas a few feet off the ground.

"Black Diamond," I cried out weakly. "Where are you?"

"Wraagh!"

I crawled forward, partially blinded by the smoke.

"Again. Guide me," I yelled and crawled toward the sound.

"Wraagh!"

When I reached her, she was lying on the floor of her cage, her black nose pressed beneath the bars, her hands squeezing metal, waiting for me, her chest heaving, gasping for breath in smoke. But her cage was locked, the heavy brass padlock a metal sentence of death.

"No. No." I screamed in rage and anger.

I dropped to the ground again, looking for something to break the lock with. I found it near the wagon wheel: a Winchester rifle that Black Diamond's attendant must have dropped. I picked it up and rammed the barrel through the lock's hasp, levered it against the bars, and pulled down, hard.

But I couldn't break it.

Arms shaking with fatigue, I tried again.

Black Diamond pressed her head against the bars. I could smell her sour smell of fear, hear her heavy breathing, see her eyes, as I jammed the barrel against the lock, the heat leaning against my back, heavy smoke now rolling over us.

Alone, I couldn't break the lock.

Matters of the Heart

These are matters of our heart.

In 1914 Edgar Rice Burroughs published *Tarzan of the Apes*, a novel of a lost English boy who, saved from death and adopted into a family of chimpanzees, spoke their own language.

The same year, Charlie Chaplin, one of America's greatest clowns, stepped into the center ring of America's attention with "Tillie's Punctured Romance," the first full-length comedy feature.

In August of 1914 the French and British stopped the Germans at the Battle of the Marne. By Christmas Eve, after five months of World War I, causalities for both sides numbered over two million, and men rested in their trenches, preparing for more death, another show in the mud.

In 1914's long summer across Kansas and into Missouri, my innocence died. Finally, I came to see the gorilla, understand at last what Jacko had meant when we first started our circus journey across the prairie. To see the gorilla in the circus means to see the darker side, to know that life is not always cotton candy and carnival rides and candied apples. In the summer of 1914, I saw the gorilla. I came to realize that life is often unfair, that America's dream of progress often destroys life and, like Harum's Colossus, rolls willy-nilly over people and animals. I also came to believe that both progress and evil come from the human heart and yet that our world is a big circus family—animals and men—and we need understanding and compassion. Maybe that's a dream, but I prefer that one to the trenches of the Marne.

Colonel Bob Thackerby also died that year, his Big Top burning around him. Rescuers found his body in the same position that I had left him, trapped beneath Old Satan's cage. For years, I tried not to think about how I had left him, and for a long time I blamed myself, called myself a murderer and worse.

Years later, I understand that I couldn't have helped him escape his trap. The fire was burning too close, and ten men could have lifted the pole to pry the wagon off. If I had stayed with him much longer, I would have fainted and died with him.

But there are memories of the heart I can't escape, cages I will never unlock. I still dream about the fire and wake in the night, screaming, cold sweat drenching my pillow and sheets. Over and over, I hear Colonel Bob's voice commanding me to help him, begging me not to leave him. Above the crackle of flames, Black Diamond's voice also calls to me. In these dreams, I smell the smoke and feel the heat and shiver at the sound of the voices. The disaster in St. Louis always ends the same way for me, many times late at night, alone, my face drenched in sweat, standing with the rifle at Black Diamond's cage. Yet, if I had to decide again tomorrow, I know what I would do in the same circumstances. I also know why in that instant when I heard Colonel Bob's command and Black Diamond's plea, together, both calling for help, I chose my friend over a man whom I once respected and whose dream of progress I too followed later in my life. But I wonder how I would have acted if I could have levered the pole. It doesn't frighten me to think what friend I would have turned to, but I'm still uneasy when I try to unlock all of the disturbing moral questions Black Diamond and Colonel Bob brought me. I don't think in these matters of the heart one key will easily fit all of our locks.

After he realized I wasn't following him, Little Wolf came back to look for me, and not finding me, he went to the menagerie. Little Wolf freed the animals from their cages, all of them. The St. Louis police and fire departments had fun chasing snakes, raccoons, horses, and Old Satan around trolley cars, through buildings, over roofs, and down alleys. Finally, they captured all of them, except four snakes and Old Satan. They finally cornered him in a schoolyard, tired, hungry, bedraggled. The police were going to shoot him until a child suggested tossing him a hunk of meat and throwing a net over him. He landed in the lion's den at the St. Louis Zoo, where he napped out his remaining days in the shade, lazily eyeing the visitors and on occasion growling.

A few days after the fire and a lot of questions from grim-faced policemen and city officials, Jacko and Little Wolf and I hitched up our wagon and a canvas-covered wagon with a team of Belgian workhorses, drove to the railroad station, and loaded our cargo on a freight train steaming west. We bounced the rails for four days and nights.

The trip was uncomfortable, rolling and pitching from the Missouri boot hills into the Kansas prairie. But they all were my circus family and we got along, in spite of all our grumbling and growling and frustration.

In the flurry after the fire, none of the officials ever bothered to peek into the canvas-covered wagon. In a way, I don't think they wanted to, or they might have been too interested in wondering why I was traveling with a black man and an Indian, or they might have been too busy trying to unravel the cause of the fire. After questions that sounded like accusations, they gave up when they discovered that we hadn't started the fire. Finally, I guess, they assumed that we were poor circus trash and left us alone.

I never saw or heard of Ripton again, but sometimes when passing graveyards in the glare of a hot day, I saw shadows like wings pointed sharply from white tombstones and imagined his dry cough.

After the train ride, we settled down on Little Wolf's ranch, on the prairie, north of Dodge City, Kansas. Jacko and Little Wolf farmed, raised cattle, and planted a huge garden every summer. They grew old together and rocked on the front porch in the evenings, spinning tales about soldiering, buffalo hunting, and Wild West shows, some of them real, some only partially made up. Every once in a while, we'd talk about the fire and how we'd escaped.

I asked Jacko how he knew to find me at Black Diamond's cage.

"Us poor freaks knows their circus family, honey," he said.

"You knew you could pull it?"

"Wagons have wheels, don't they?" he asked.

153

We built a huge cage for Black Diamond on the bottom floor of our stock barn. Black Diamond and I spent a lot of time together. I played with her, studied her, tried to understand her language, and wrote in a journal my observations about the circus and Black Diamond. Once, remembering how Little Wolf and I had saved her from the greenhouse, I tried to talk Little Wolf into letting her go into the house. He refused, saying he couldn't listen to the Old Ones with a four-hundred-pound gorilla breaking furniture and chomping violet leaves.

I enrolled in the Dodge City High School and worked for old Doc Rowe, a local veterinarian, after school and during the summers. I started saving my Indian head pennies and buffalo nickels for college, but I didn't think I had much chance to study science and had about given up my dreams when the vet wrote a letter to one of his friends in Manhattan, Kansas. One of them, a professor from Kansas State Agricultural College, braved a March blizzard to talk to me and read my journal entries about Black Diamond. A few weeks later, I received a scholarship offer to study zoology at the college.

In 1923, my name changed to Dr. Samantha Puluski when I received my Ph.D. in zoology. Jacko sent me a short congratulatory note for my accomplishments. Its shaky handwriting read: "Wraagh." I studied vocalization and signing in gorillas, and I became an authority on primate behaviors and language. Now, I teach zoology at the university and work with zoos across the country, advising them on the proper care of gorillas. Recently, the Zoological Society of London published a paper of mine on primate communication. I also volunteer my time with a group that rescues mistreated animals from circuses and traveling side shows. We'd found a lot of pathetic cases, like the case of baboon chained so long in his small cage that his flesh had grown over his chain.

If Jacko and Little Wolf were alive today, they'd shake their heads at the clouds of madness forming once again in Europe as Hitler wants to make Germany into a cage of hate and misery. This is a country that up to 1939 pioneered in zoological gardens and primate studies. Jacko died of cancer a year after I received my degree, a shrivelled-up black man, unafraid of death at the end, with a smile on his face for me, in the Old Soldiers Home in Ft. Dodge, Kansas. I made it back to his bedside to thank him for being one of my two fathers. He's buried in the Ft. Dodge cemetery, an old military cemetery, under a spreading elm tree, beneath a white tombstone, at rest with other buffalo soldiers from the 10th Cavalry.

My other father disappeared from the farm the year after Jacko died. He vanished on a crystalline October day, an Indian summer day with fleecy clouds and sunlight like gold. One day, checking on him for me, the sheriff's office found an empty house, clean, with everything in order, except for a missing roan horse. After haphazardly searching for him for a few days, the sheriff declared him to be a missing person. I think Little Wolf would have appreciated the irony of the comment, feeling the way he did about how America worked hard to ignore Indians. When I was looking through the farmhouse in Kansas, I couldn't find his ceremonial clothing—his war bonnet and buckskin clothing and medicine bag—so I think he rode off to die, to lose himself in the wind and grass and thunderstorms of the prairie, to leave his bones for prairie wolves.

Black Diamond died before I went away to the university, on a May day, rich with the smell of dogwood and bright with the red of redbuds, peacefully, her brown eyes sparkling until she closed them and relaxed. At last, she was free, out of her cage, and I held her hand, unafraid, my heart shattered in grief. As white thunderheads stacked up in the west, I hitched a horse to her body and dragged her to a high knoll. There I wrapped her in my horse blanket and buried her on a high spot, her grayed head turned toward her Africa, overlooking the Kansas prairie as a meadow lark trilled and a hawk soared, riding wind currents high overhead.

Every few years, I go back to western Kansas, to visit the grave of Jacko, to hear the wind and the coyotes barking under a velvet sky, to sit on the knoll with Black Diamond. There I remember my circus family and what they taught me. There I listen to memories of our hearts, which still beat in me.

HOW TO ORDER THIS NOVEL
Paperback Edition: ISBN 0-9656007-0-X

Please send me _____ copy(s) of *Heart of a Gorilla*.	
Price for each paperback book: $8.95:	_____
Shipping and handling for each book, $1.25:	_____
North Dakota residents add $.54 sales tax for each book:	_____
Total:	_____

Please make checks payable to The Buffalo Commons Press. Send to P.O. Box 525, Dickinson, North Dakota, 58601-0525 For telephone orders, call (701)-227-2145 or (701)-225-2473.